The (Mostly) True Story of
CLEOPATRA'S NEEDLE

The (Mostly) True Story of
CLEOPATRA'S NEEDLE

BY
DAN GUTMAN

HOLIDAY HOUSE   NEW YORK

ACKNOWLEDGMENTS

Special thanks to Dr. Bob Brier, Mary Galbaski, Bryan Godwin, Rich Jacobson, Frank Lovece, Andrew Ross, Karen Gray Ruelle, Amy Toth, John Simko, Laura Kincaid, Nina Wallace, Howard Wolf, and all the folks at Holiday House.

Text copyright © 2024 by Dan Gutman
Maps copyright © 2024 by Nina Wallace
Illustrations copyright © 2024 by Kelley McMorris
All rights reserved. No part of this book may be reproduced, transmitted, or stored in an information retrieval system in any form or by any means, graphic, electronic, or mechanical, including photocopying, taping, and recording, without prior written permission from the publisher. Additionally, no part of this book may be used or reproduced in any manner for the purpose of training artificial intelligence technologies or systems, nor for text and data mining.
HOLIDAY HOUSE is registered in the U.S. Patent and Trademark Office.
Printed and bound in July 2025 at Sheridan, Chelsea, MI, USA.
www.holidayhouse.com
First Paperback Edition
3 5 7 9 10 8 6 4 2 (hardcover)
1 3 5 7 9 10 8 6 4 2 (paperback)

Credits: Vintage photos and artwork were found through the New York Public Library, the Library of Congress, the Metropolitan Museum of Art, and other sources. The contemporary photos are by Dan Gutman.

Library of Congress Cataloging-in-Publication Data
Names: Gutman, Dan, author.
Title: The (mostly) true story of Cleopatra's needle / by Dan Gutman.
Description: First edition. | New York : Holiday House, 2024.
Audience: Ages 8-12. | Audience: Grades 4-6. | Summary: "Five kids across centuries recount the history of Cleopatra's Needle, from its construction in ancient Egypt to moving it across the ocean to New York City in the 19th century"—Provided by publisher.
Identifiers: LCCN 2023024655 | ISBN 9780823454846 (hardcover)
Subjects: CYAC: Cleopatra's Needle (New York, N.Y.)—Fiction. Obelisks—Fiction. | LCGFT: Historical fiction. | Novels.
Classification: LCC PZ7.G9846 Mog 2024 | DDC [Fic]—dc23
LC record available at https://lccn.loc.gov/2023024655

ISBN: 978-0-8234-5484-6 (hardcover)
ISBN: 978-0-8234-6180-6 (paperback)

EU Authorized Representative: HackettFlynn Ltd, 36 Cloch Choirneal, Balrothery, Co. Dublin, K32 C942, Ireland. EU@walkerpublishinggroup.com

To Elizabeth Law

CONTENTS

INTRODUCTION   1

PART 1: I AM ENSLAVED. THIS IS MY STORY.
1461–1460 BCE
Diary of Zosar Zuberi, a boy in Aswan, Egypt,
where Cleopatra's Needle was carved (Translated
from Egyptian)   7

PART 2: I AM AN ARTIST. THIS IS MY STORY.
1459 BCE
Diary of Lateef Jabari, a boy in Heliopolis, Egypt,
where Cleopatra's Needle was raised for the first time
(Translated from Egyptian)   29

PART 3: I AM A SPY. THIS IS MY STORY.
1879–1880
Diary of Panya Hassan, a girl in Alexandria, Egypt,
who witnessed Cleopatra's Needle being taken away
from Egypt (Translated from Arabic)   57

PART 4: I AM A STOWAWAY. THIS IS MY STORY.
1880
Diary of Thomas Brighton, a boy on the ship
that brought Cleopatra's Needle to America 99

PART 5: I AM AN INVENTOR. THIS IS MY STORY.
1879–1881
Diary of Rebecca Watson, a girl in New York City
who witnessed Cleopatra's Needle being brought
to Central Park 135

FACTS AND FICTIONS
Everything in this book is true, except for the stuff
I made up. It's only fair to tell you which is which. 187

The (Mostly) True Story of
CLEOPATRA'S NEEDLE

INTRODUCTION

Let me just say from the start that I didn't want to do this. I didn't want to have *anything* to do with this book.

To be honest, I don't particularly like reading books and I'm not crazy about learning stuff or going to museums or becoming well-rounded or any of that other boring stuff that nice boys are supposed to like.

I didn't ask to come here. I just wanted to stay home and watch a ball game on TV. My mom made me come.

So here I am—in Central Park, in New York City. It's probably the most famous park in the world, and there's lots of cool stuff to do here. Like, they've got a zoo and two skating rinks and a carousel and rocks to climb and ball fields and all kinds of other fun stuff. But no, my mom didn't take me to see any of that cool stuff. She took me *here*.

Cleopatra's Needle in Central Park today.

We're sitting on a wooden bench in front of this giant...thing. Mom calls it "Cleopatra's Needle." It's this big monument made out of stone, I guess. It looks sort of like the Washington Monument, with that point at the top. I said that to my mother, hoping we could move on and be done with it. But she kept right on talking.

"Cleopatra's Needle is an *obelisk*," she told me. "The Washington Monument is not an obelisk."

Well, excuse *me*! I never heard of an obelisk. I always called it a "pointy thing." Apparently, you can't call something an obelisk if it's made from a bunch of blocks put together. An obelisk has to be just one solid piece of stone. Doesn't seem like a big difference to me.

"Just *look* at it!" my mom said as she gazed up in wonder. "It's the height of a seven-story building, but it was carved three thousand five hundred years ago! It's the oldest outdoor monument in New York City and the oldest man-made object in Central Park, one of the oldest in the *world*! And we're sitting right in front of it. Can you believe it? It's like an ancient skyscraper."

"I really don't care, Mom."

I know it was obnoxious. But spending a Saturday

going to see some big old pointy rock is not exactly my idea of a good time.

Still. *Three thousand five hundred years.* That's some old chunk of rock, I had to admit. I know that World War II was in the 1940s. That was less than a century ago. I know that the Civil War was in the 1860s. So that was like a hundred and fifty years ago. The Declaration of Independence was 1776. That's about as far back as my mind can imagine. I can't wrap my head around something that's thirty-five centuries old.

Cleopatra's Needle had some weird ancient symbols carved into the sides. So I guess it's from prehistoric times or whatever. But I wasn't going to ask any specifics, because my mom would go into a long history of the thing and I'd be stuck having to be here for hours.

"It was carved in 1461 BCE," my mom told me.

So what? Just because something is old doesn't mean I need to care about it. Mom's always trying to get me interested in the stuff that *she's* interested in. I'm not falling for that old trick. Nobody tells me what I should be interested in.

Mom takes us places. We live in New Jersey. It's not that far to get on a train or bus into New York, so we go to the city from time to time. She means well, but unless it's a game or the Thanksgiving Day parade or something cool, I just don't care.

My sister had to go to a birthday party today, so Mom took me to the Metropolitan Museum of Art in New York. I had to look at a bunch of sculptures and paintings and stuff—yawn. The place goes on *forever*. Afterward we got hot dogs from a vendor on the street and she took me to Cleopatra's Needle. It's right behind the museum, in Central Park.

"This obelisk weighs about two hundred and twenty *tons*," Mom explained. "The pedestal alone is fifty tons."

She started rattling off statistics, the way she does. She likes numbers.

"It's sixty-nine feet high," she said. "And each side is eight feet across."

"That's fascinating, Mom," I said semi-sarcastically. "Can we go now?"

"Of course, there wasn't a *city* here in 1461 BCE," Mom continued. "This obelisk was carved in Egypt, in a place called Aswan. It's about five hundred miles south of Cairo...."

Did I mention that my mom makes her living as

a storyteller? She goes to schools and fairs and tells stories. Not just for kids. For everybody. She does the voices of all the different characters and everything. She really knows how to suck you into a story. Sometimes they're true stories. Sometimes she just makes stuff up.

Anyway, I have to sit through her stories all the time. She considers it a challenge to try to get me hooked.

"Think about it," she said. "People in ancient Egypt carved this giant obelisk out of solid granite. Then in 1880, somebody managed to load it onto a boat. Then they brought it all the way across the Atlantic Ocean. Then they unloaded it at the Hudson River. Then they dragged it across Manhattan and stood it up right here. And remember, back then they didn't have trucks, airplanes, computers..."

I had to fight my temptation to ask her how it was possible to do all that stuff with old technology.

"There's a secret hidden inside Cleopatra's Needle, you know," Mom told me.

Okay, I'll bite. I can't resist a secret.

"What's the secret?" I asked.

"Oh, so *now* you're interested?" she said. "It starts a long time ago, in Africa...."

PART 1

I AM ENSLAVED. THIS IS MY STORY.

(1461–1460 BCE)

Diary of Zosar Zuberi, a boy in Aswan, Egypt, where Cleopatra's Needle was carved
Translated from Egyptian

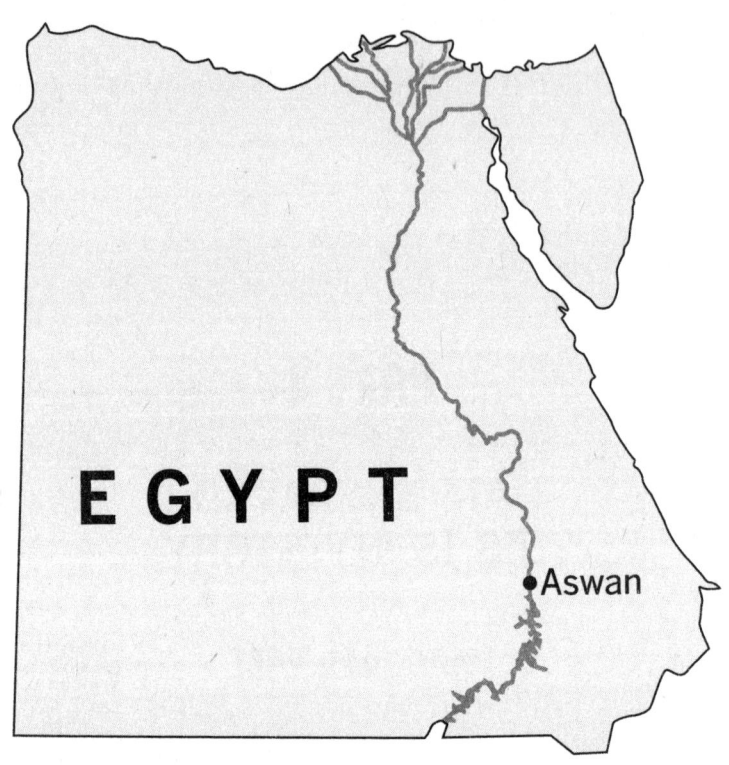

Obelisks were carved at the granite quarry in Aswan, Egypt.

DAY 1

We were rudely awakened in the middle of the night by our master. He told us to pack our things immediately. Why are we being taken away? I have done nothing wrong. My family has always obeyed the rules. Why are they doing this to us? This is our home.

DAY 2

We were put on a boat and taken to Aswan. Mother, father, and all three of my sisters. I don't know why we have been moved. Is this a punishment? I don't know what we have done. My little sister, Nakia, has been crying all morning.

Every time there is a knock on the door in the middle of the night, we know we will be moving. We go where we are told. At least our family will be allowed to stay together this time.

DAY 3

We arrived by boat on the Nile to Aswan. I think I know why we were taken here. This is where the quarries are. Aswan has the best pink granite in all the world. Huge blocks of it. The granite is used to make monuments and statues, which are brought to all parts of Egypt for people to admire.

My father has worked as a stonecutter. He is very good at carving granite. His services must be needed. I am just glad the rest of us are allowed to be with him. But I am afraid the masters are going to put me to work too this time. I just celebrated my birthday number nine. So now I am a man. I am capable of lifting heavy objects and working long hours under the hot sun. I am a hard worker and will do a good job, because I do not want to be whipped.

DAY 4

We have been put in temporary quarters. There is no roof, but that will not be a problem because rain hardly ever comes. We have been told, as we expected, that my father and I will work in the quarry. My mother and sisters have been assigned to work the fields. We start first thing tomorrow morning. I have never carved stone before. It looks like very hard work. My father says he will teach me.

DAY 5

Father and I were taken on a long march to the quarry. It must be a very large project that we will be working on. There are hundreds, maybe thousands of workers here. Many of them are paid laborers who work the fields during the growing season, and then come to Aswan to work in the quarry during the remainder of the year. Many others are prisoners who have been convicted of committing crimes. A boy who looked like he was my age told me his uncle took a piece of fruit that did not belong to him and was sentenced to five years of hard labor in Aswan.

Many others are enslaved people, like us. Years ago, my parents were taken captive during a war in Syria and brought to Egypt. Their heads were shaved and they were branded with the pharaoh's name. The children of an enslaved person are also enslaved, so I am a slave.

I have never been able to understand how it is possible for one human being to own another human being. How can that be right? My father says that is the way it has always been, and that is the way it will always be. So I should get used to it.

DAY 6

We were introduced to the overseer. His name is Yamu-nedjeh. He looks like a very mean man and he spoke roughly to us. He demands total obedience and promises punishment if we disobey. The masters are always mean men. I suppose you have to be mean if you are going to be a master.

Yamu-nedjeh told us why we have been brought here. The pharaoh, Thutmosis III, has tasked us to carve a large obelisk out of the granite. I did not know what an obelisk was, but my father whispered the answer to me. An obelisk is a long, four-sided monument that slopes gradually from its base and comes to a point at the top.

I do not understand. Why is making an obelisk so important to the pharaoh? There are so many workers here. Could not our labors be put to better use if we were assigned to grow crops and feed the hungry people of Egypt? That is what I would do if I were pharaoh. I would try to make life better for my people.

It seems to be a waste of time and energy to have hundreds of men make a stone monument that serves no purpose except that it will be pleasant to look at. But my father says to keep such views to myself if I do not want to be punished. I am not here to think, he says. I am here to work.

DAY 7

It is very hot, dry, and dusty in Aswan. It will not be easy to work outside all day. My father said it is going to take a very long time to carve an obelisk out of granite. He says I may be twelve or thirteen years old by the time we are finished. That is okay with me, but I feel sorry for him. Father is thirty-five years now, so he is an old man. Few people live to reach the number fifty. Working out in the sun is no way to spend your final years.

Father does not like to talk about what happened to his hand. But I know. He had finished eating his rations, but he was still hungry. So he took another man's fish and he was caught. There was talk of executing him, but instead they cut off the fourth finger of his left hand. My father was allowed to live only because he is a skilled stone carver. This all happened before the year of my birth.

It is hard to work with stone when you don't have all your fingers. But Father told me he has gotten used to it and that I should not feel sorry for him. Our family lives on, he says. The sun, thank Ra, still shines. We still breathe air. Other slaves have not been so lucky. Father said I should feel sorry for all the ones who have died. And I do. But I feel sorry for my father too.

DAY 8

There is very good news! Father told me he made a deal with Yamu-nedjeh. When we finish carving the obelisk, he will no longer be enslaved. My father will be free! I asked him why Yamu-nedjeh would make such a deal. He told me that Yamu-nedjeh expects him to work harder and faster if he knows he will be freed when the job is done. I will work hard and fast too. I also want to be free as soon as possible.

DAY 9

I accompanied my father and other workers to the quarry. Before we can carve the obelisk, it is important to select the correct piece of granite. Aswan has excellent pink granite, but some parts of the quarry are better than others. For a large obelisk we must find a section of granite that has no flaws or cracks in it. They do not want us to spend months and years working on an obelisk and then find out it was damaged.

Yamu-nedjeh chose a spot in the quarry. It was then washed down with water from the Nile to clean the surface, and we got ready to start working. But my father noticed a tiny crack in the granite, and he pointed it out. Yamu-nedjeh was angry that his judgment was questioned. He had a worker drill a test hole, and he discovered that Father was right. There was a crack in the granite.

Father found another location that was more suitable for carving. It is on the edge of the quarry. That is good because it is closer to the Nile, which means it will be easier to move the obelisk to a boat when we are finished carving it.

DAY 10

We began carving the obelisk today. Father and some of the other workers used animal fat and charcoal to draw the shape of the obelisk on the granite. I counted off seventy paces as I walked the entire length. Someday, when they stand the obelisk up, it is going to be very tall.

One hundred thirty of us were positioned shoulder to shoulder around the outline that had been drawn on the granite. Then each of us was given a black rock, round and about the size of my head. The rock is called dolerite. It is very heavy and very hard, harder than granite.

We were ordered to raise the dolerite over our head and slam it down against the surface of the granite. When I smashed my dolerite down, some flakes of granite flew off. Father told me that meant I was doing it right.

Yamu-nedjeh clapped out a rhythm with his hands and all one hundred thirty of us slammed our dolerite against the granite. Over and over and over again. It was very hard to keep up the pace. Sweat was pouring off my face and pooling up on the stone below me. Every few minutes a worker came by with a broom to sweep away the sweat and the granite dust we had created.

We worked until the sun disappeared from the sky, each of us pounding our stone against the granite repeatedly. At that point Yamu-nedjeh stopped clapping. I looked around to see we had made a smooth groove about one inch deep around the outline of the obelisk. Father said that was a good day's work.

Yamu-nedjeh inspected the stone again to make sure there weren't any cracks in it. If he found any, we would have had to start all over again tomorrow. Luckily, there were no cracks.

Bending and squatting all day is hard work. Breathing in granite dust made us cough and gasp for breath. Father came home sore and exhausted. So did I. My arm and shoulder muscles were in terrible pain. Mother rubbed oil on us to make us feel better, but it did not help very much. We went to sleep immediately.

DAY 11

Back to the quarry to pound the dolerite today. Now there is a two-inch trench around the outline of the obelisk. At one inch per day, we are going to be here for a very long time. I am tired and sick of this work already. But we must continue. We have no choice but to do what we are told or suffer the lash.

DAY 12

More pounding the dolerite today. I am afraid that I am going to die at a very young age.

DAY 13

More pounding the dolerite today. The other workers say that when we finish making the obelisk, it will be floated down the Nile to the city of Heliopolis in the north. So we do all the work and the people of Heliopolis get to enjoy it. That does not seem fair to me. Father told me that life is not fair, so stop complaining.

DAY 14

More pounding the dolerite today. While we were working, Asim, one of the older slaves working next to me, whispered in my ear that we should rise up and fight back against the masters. Asim said we cannot fail. There are hundreds of us, and only a few of them.

But I reminded him that we have no weapons, and that Yamu-nedjeh carries a long sword with him at all times. Asim said that if a bunch of us charged at Yamu-nedjeh, we could overpower him and take away his sword. Then we would be free. I replied, "You go first and we will see what happens." Asim didn't say anything after that.

Working on the obelisk is a hard life, especially for older men like Asim. My mother says maybe we should run away. But run away to where? We would surely be caught. The masters might remove our fingers or toes. More likely, we would be executed.

Father reminded her that once the obelisk is completed, he will be rewarded with his freedom, and we will be able to live the life we choose. I cannot even imagine what it would be like to be free. I do not know what we would do if we did not have a master telling us when to work, when to sleep, or when to eat.

DAY 52
More pounding the dolerite.

Asim died today. I saw it. He raised up his dolerite and fell over dead. He was replaced by another slave as soon as he hit the ground. We continued working.

DAY 547
For a year and a half, we have been pounding the granite with dolerite. Every day, the trench we are digging around the obelisk becomes an inch deeper. We are working completely below the surface of the quarry now. The obelisk is beginning to look like an obelisk, laying on its side. It is becoming a beautiful thing.

When we started, I was a boy. Now I feel like an old man. But I have strong muscles in my arms and legs, which is a good thing.

DAY 550
The obelisk is nearly finished. Our next task will be to free it from the quarry. We are now

tunneling below it from both sides, which is even harder to do. I was afraid the obelisk might fall on top of us as we chipped away the remaining pieces of granite. But as soon as we created a hole that went underneath the obelisk, a long granite block was put in the hole to support it. We will keep pounding the dolerite underneath until the obelisk is completely freed from the quarry.

Another prisoner died today. I did not know his name. They carried his body away and we were told to keep working.

DAY 551

While some workers continued carving out the bottom of the obelisk, the rest of us were tasked with making the other three sides perfectly straight and smooth. We were each given a small block of stone. Wet sand and granite flakes were applied to the surface of the obelisk and we were told to rub our stone against the obelisk over and over again. Yamu-nedjeh clapped out a rhythm. This is not as hard work as pounding the obelisk with dolerite, but it is still hard, dull work.

DAY 552
We polished the obelisk today.

DAY 553
Polished the obelisk.

DAY 554
Same as yesterday. More polishing.

DAY 611
Today is the big day! After almost two years of working, today the giant obelisk is to be freed from the ground from which it has been held since the beginning of time. That also means that very soon Father will be freed from his servitude.

The polishing is complete. The obelisk is very smooth now. I have been wondering how we were going to pull it out of the quarry. Today I got the answer. During the last week, workers delivered many long, thick wooden planks. Each one is the height of a small tree. I don't know where the wood came from. There are few trees in Aswan.

These heavy planks were placed all around the obelisk, with one end jammed underneath and the other end sticking out of the ground. I counted twenty planks on each side. We were ordered to grab hold at the end of the nearest plank.

"Pull!" shouted Yamu-nedjeh.

We pulled down on the top end of the planks. Nothing happened.

"Pull harder!" shouted Yamu-nedjeh.

We pulled down harder. I didn't think anything was going to happen, but suddenly we were able to pull our plank down, and the obelisk rose up out of the ground that had held it. It seemed like a miracle to me. How could mere human beings lift such a large and heavy object? We were all proud of our accomplishment. You could see it in the men's eyes as the giant obelisk rose up. It is freed from the quarry, much like my family will be free very soon.

DAY 612

Now the harder work begins. We must drag the obelisk to the Nile, where it will be floated to Heliopolis. After we raised the obelisk above the quarry surface, pieces of discarded granite were placed underneath it to hold it off the ground.

Then hundreds more workers arrived, some of them with ropes, animal fat, water, and oxen. Other men brought a huge wooden sled they had built. They positioned the sled in front of the obelisk. The sled was covered with water and animal grease. Ropes were attached to the obelisk. All of us—hundreds of workers plus the oxen—were ordered to go to the front of the sled. My father positioned himself next to me.

"Pull!" shouted Yamu-nedjeh.

The obelisk did not move. Yamu-nedjeh ordered workers to put more grease on the sled.

While they were doing that, an idea came into my head. I told my father that we would be able to move the obelisk more easily if a round object was inserted under it. We could, for example, take many round stones and roll the obelisk onto the sled instead of sliding it.

Father looked at me for a long time before answering.

"We are enslaved people," he reminded me. "You are not here to think. You are here to work."

And that was the end of that idea. It took all day, but we finally pulled the obelisk onto the sled.

DAY 613

The Nile is a short distance from the granite quarry. It would have been much easier and faster to bring the obelisk to the river if we had taken my suggestion and rolled it there. But that was not to be. Instead, Yamu-nedjeh gathered hundreds of us to push, pull ropes, and drag the sled with the obelisk on it up the small hill to the river. We worked all day under the hot sun to move it a few feet as oil, grease, and water were spread on the dirt in front. Another worker died.

DAY 620

We spent seven days dragging the obelisk to the river. I was not aware, but while we were carving the obelisk hundreds of other laborers were building a wooden barge at the edge of the Nile. It is the largest vessel I have ever seen. It will hold the obelisk as it floats down the Nile to Heliopolis.

Dozens of smaller boats were tied to the barge. I counted thirty. These boats will be paddled down the river to tow and guide the barge.

With great effort, we slid the obelisk onto the barge. I looked at it in wonder and thought, it will be impossible for this barge, as large as it is, to keep the obelisk afloat. It is sure to sink under the tremendous weight. If that happens, all our work of the last two years will be for nothing.

But the barge did not sink. Yamu-nedjeh gave the order, and the barge pulled away from the shore.

"Farewell!" we shouted as the obelisk floated away on the Nile. We watched and cheered until it was too far away to see anymore.

Finally, our job is finished. Hundreds of us had worked very hard under very difficult conditions. We created a beautiful object, and for that we are proud, even if we will not be able to enjoy it. Many innocent men died. Father, fortunately, did not. He will finally be a free man. We will be a free family. This calls for a celebration. We will sleep late tomorrow morning and enjoy our new freedom.

DAY 621

We were awakened from a deep sleep by pounding and shouting voices.

"What is it?" my mother asked as we struggled to get out of bed in the darkness. It was Yamu-nedjeh and some other overseers.

"Get up!" he yelled. "You are late!"

Father looked at me and put his finger to his lips to tell me not to talk back. But I could not help myself.

"We were promised our freedom!" I complained. "You told my father that when the obelisk is finished we would no longer be enslaved! You promised! The obelisk is finished! We should be free!"

Yamu-nedjeh looked at me with both anger and amusement in his eyes.

"You are a slave," he finally said. "We start on a new obelisk today. Get to work!"

MEANWHILE, IN THE PRESENT DAY...

"I really don't care, Mom," I said after she finished telling the story about the kid who helped carve Cleopatra's Needle. It must have really sucked to be enslaved, but once Mom gets started telling her stories, there's no stopping her.

I wasn't just being obnoxious. I really didn't care. So they carved the obelisk in ancient Egypt. Big deal. They carved lots of stuff in ancient Egypt. The museum was filled with all the stuff they carved. I get it. The ancient Egyptians were really good at working with stone.

In the back of my mind, I was wondering how they could have possibly brought a two-hundred-twenty-ton obelisk from Egypt all the way to America. But I didn't want to ask because that would just encourage my mother to tell another story. If we left now, I could still catch the second half of the game.

"Let me just tell you how they stood this thing up for the first time in Egypt," she said. "It won't take long. Then we'll go home. Promise."

PART 2

I AM AN ARTIST.
THIS IS MY STORY.

(1459 BCE)

*Diary of Lateef Jabari, a boy in Heliopolis, Egypt, where
Cleopatra's Needle was raised for the first time*
Translated from Egyptian

Thutmosis III.

DAY 1

Do you like this picture? I drew it. It is a picture of Thutmosis III, the great warrior king and pharaoh of all Egypt. I made it by myself and I think it is a very good likeness.

I have never seen the pharaoh with my own eyes. He lives in Cairo. But this is what I imagine him to look like. I wish I could see the pharaoh in person. Maybe someday I will see him and give him this picture to honor him. That is my dream.

I am smaller than most eleven-year-old boys. When they play their rough games, I stand on the side and watch. I do not know how to play. I do not want to get hurt. And I am not interested in playing games, anyway. I told my mother that I will grow up and create great works of art.

"Lateef, that cannot happen," my mother told me. She said people do not grow up to draw pictures. They grow up and work in the fields or in the quarries. Or they tend to the animals. Or they build pyramids and other things for our people. She said you cannot support a family by drawing pictures. People do not grow up and make art.

"Maybe I will be the first," I said.

Mother shook her head sadly. She says that when I get older, I will be put to work like everyone else. Until then, I am free to waste my time drawing pictures, if that makes me happy.

It does.

DAY 2

Do you like my new picture? I drew it yesterday. I know it is not very good. Maybe I will make a better one.

This is an obelisk. Not everyone knows what the word "obelisk" means. An obelisk looks something like a pyramid that has been stretched out so that it is much taller and thinner.

Obelisks look like stretched-out pyramids.

Pyramids are much more famous than obelisks, but I like obelisks better. Pyramids represent death and dying and sadness. They are built to be tombs for the pharaohs. But obelisks represent life. They point toward the sun. Heliopolis, the place where I live, is called the City of the Sun.

We call the sun Ra. Ra gives us life, strength, health, and happiness. All creatures are alive because of the light from Ra. We could not exist without it. So each day we face the heavenly orb in the sky and pray, asking Ra to continue giving us the gift of life on earth. We make obelisks and point them to the sky to honor Ra.

Think of it—the path of Ra across the sky is like the life of a person. It is a baby in the morning, a youth in the middle of the day, and an old person at night. And then the light of Ra goes away until the next day, when the process begins once again.

But that is not why I drew the picture of an obelisk. There is big news that I have just heard—a large obelisk is due to arrive in Heliopolis from the granite quarries of Aswan. This is true. It will take a number of days to get here. I am filled with anticipation.

They floated the obelisk down the Nile River to Heliopolis.

My mother does not like my pictures. She told me to stop drawing them. She does not want anyone to see that I waste so much time making pictures. I love to draw and I will continue drawing my pictures. But I will hide them under my bed so she will not see them.

DAY 3

I have more exciting news to report. Perhaps this is rumor and perhaps it is fact. But I have heard that the pharaoh, Thutmosis III, is coming to Heliopolis!

I can barely believe the words I have just written. The pharaoh, the great Thutmosis III, the son of Ra, the son of the sun, the king of Upper and Lower Egypt, the military genius, the powerful and glorious god on earth who gives all life, stability, and strength is coming to Heliopolis! He is coming here to witness the raising of his obelisk on our shores and to celebrate his third decade of reign.

Praise be to Thutmosis III and praise be to me, for I will be able to see the pharaoh with my own eyes. This is my dream come true.

I know much about the pharaoh. Thutmosis III is a builder of temples, palaces, and monuments, and he became the sixth pharaoh of the Eighteenth

Dynasty when he was just two years old. He has built fifty temples, captured more than three hundred cities, and created the largest empire Egypt has ever known.

I still cannot believe the pharaoh is coming here.

Sadly, I have other news to report. Mother found the drawings I had hidden under my bed. She was very angry and threw all my papyrus out the window.

But I do not care. I will have the opportunity to see the pharaoh Thutmosis III in person. Maybe I will get more papyrus and draw his picture.

DAY 7

The pharaoh has not yet come to Heliopolis. But it was a glorious day nevertheless. For today, our obelisk arrived. It was carved in Aswan, far to the south.

As word spread of its arrival, hundreds of citizens gathered on the banks of the Nile to greet our new monument. Thirty boats were seen first. They used the current of the river to tow a barge with the obelisk lying on top of a huge wooden sled. Many men were needed to steer the barge so it would not bump into the river banks.

And then the obelisk came into view. What a sight! It was lying on its side on top of the barge. It is so big. I cannot imagine how the stone carvers of Aswan were able to cut such a large piece of granite and lift it out of the quarry.

The labors of hundreds of strong men were needed to pull the obelisk off the barge. Using ropes, they dragged it onto the shore next to the Temple of the Sun. That is where it will one day stand, and pilgrims will be able to come here and worship the pharaoh long after his death.

I do not know how they are going to stand the obelisk upright. It must be so heavy. It will probably take the effort of a thousand of our strongest men.

Even lying on its side, the obelisk is a beautiful thing to look at. Standing up, it will attract attention to our city. It will also serve a useful purpose. As the sun, Ra, passes overhead, the obelisk will cast a moving shadow across the ground. That will tell us how much of the day has passed and how much of the day remains.

DAY 8

The most amazing event happened this morning. A man I had never seen before came to our door. He announced himself as "Omari," which means "high born." This man Omari was wearing an official-looking robe, and he said he had something very important to discuss. Mother immediately fell to her knees and began to weep and beg.

"I didn't do anything," she sobbed. "If I did something wrong I am truly sorry. It will never happen again. For that you have my promise."

"Stand up, woman," Omari told her. "It is not you I am interested in. It is your son."

"What did Lateef do?" my mother asked, wrapping her arms around me protectively. "Please do not take my son away. I beg of you."

"Come with me, Lateef," Omari said simply, grabbing my wrist.

"No!"

My mother sobbed as I was taken away. I was afraid I would never see her again. I was afraid of the punishment for whatever crime I may have committed. Perhaps I was going to be executed. I was sweating and crying.

Omari took me to a building where another man was waiting to speak to me. He was sitting behind a table and he looked like he was very important, but I did not know who he was.

I was trembling with fear. Before the man spoke, I looked at his table. The papyrus that my mother had thrown out the window was on it—drawings of the pharaoh, obelisks, and other things.

"Is your name Lateef?" he asked.

"Yes," I said, keeping my eyes on the floor.

"What is this?" he asked, picking up one of the pages.

"Pictures," I replied.

"Did you draw these pictures, Lateef?"

"I did," I admitted. "Was that wrong? What will my punishment be?"

"They were found in the street," he replied.

I did not know what to say. Perhaps it is against the law to throw papyrus on the street. I said nothing and waited for my punishment.

"You are quite good at drawing pictures, Lateef," he said.

I exhaled. Perhaps I would not be punished after all.

"Thank you."

"The pharaoh wants you to make some drawings," he told me.

I could not believe my ears. Drawings for the pharaoh? Me?

"What kind of drawings?" I asked.

"The pharaoh wants you to draw the hieroglyphs that will be carved into the obelisk."

Hieroglyphs are the pictures that are used to turn our thoughts into writing. I cannot believe my good fortune. Of all the citizens of Heliopolis, I have been chosen to draw the hieroglyphs that will be inscribed on the four sides of the obelisk! Why me? I do not know. Perhaps it is hard to find people who are good at drawing pictures.

When I returned home, my mother took hold of me and would not let go. She was so relieved that I was alive. When I told her the good news, she did not believe me at first. But finally I was able to convince her. She even said that she would get me more papyrus to draw on.

"Maybe now you will stop throwing my drawings out the window," I told her.

"If I had not thrown your drawings out the window," she replied, "the pharaoh would never have noticed your ability to make pictures."

True, I suppose.

DAY 9

The next day that man Omari came to our door again. This time my mother did not cry. Omari told me he had come to explain what I will need to draw.

"The obelisk is not just a tribute to the sun, Ra," he told me. "It is also a tribute to the pharaoh. Thutmosis III is the son of the sun. The obelisk will be a monument proclaiming the glory of his conquests and a testament to his accomplishments."

He told me exactly what the pharaoh wished me to say with my pictures, not that I had any idea what it meant....

> The Horus, Strong-Bull-Appearing-In-Thebes, he of the Two La Goddesses, Enduring-of-kingship-like-Ra-in-heaven, Bodily son of Atum, whom the Mistress of Heliopolis bore to him, Thutmosis, whom they created in the temple in the beauty

of their members, knowing that he would exercise enduring kingship throughout eternity, the King of Upper and Lower Egypt, Men-kheper-ra, beloved of Atum, the great god, together with his Enneat, granted all life, stability, and dominion like Ra for ever.

There is more, but that is the general idea. I can draw the words, but still don't understand what they mean.

"Get to work, Lateef," Omari ordered me before leaving.

DAY 10

This is a big job that will require many drawings. I will work very hard to make sure my pictures match the meaning of the words the pharaoh wishes to convey.

Do you like my new drawing? It took me many hours to complete. These are some of the elements I will be using for the inscriptions on the sides of the obelisk. I am so excited to think that my pictures will be given to the stone carvers and they will carve them into the obelisk.

We use hieroglyphs to turn words into pictures.

DAY 15

I have completed half the drawings required. Every day I go to the Temple of the Sun to deliver new pictures to Omari and then watch the sculptors carving them into the obelisk. I can see it is easier for them to do their job when the obelisk is lying on its side than if they were to do it after it is standing up. But they will have to wait to do the final side, because that side is lying face down.

It is going to be beautiful when the carving is done. People are already coming from all over Egypt to look at the obelisk. The sculptors are working very hard. They know that if they make one small mistake, they will be flogged.

DAY 16

When I was at the Temple of the Sun today, I saw something unusual. Hundreds of workers were outside the temple digging with shovels. Surely they are not planning to place the obelisk underground. That is where it came from in the first place.

I watched as they dug up dirt and sand, then carried it and piled it up to make a hill next to the bottom part of the obelisk. Very strange.

DAY 17

Omari told me why the workers are building the giant sand hill. They are going to use that hill to help stand up the obelisk. I do not understand how they are going to do that, but Omari says it will all become clear.

DAY 20

My obelisk drawings are finished. I am very proud of my work. After I delivered each drawing to Omari, he gave his approval. Sometimes he would ask me to make a small change in the drawing, which I did. The stone carvers work very fast. Soon they will be finished with their carvings and the obelisk will be raised.

DAY 25

Big news! The pharaoh Thutmosis III has arrived! He has come here to witness the raising of his obelisk. I have heard that the pharaoh has even brought one of his sons with him. Tomorrow will be the big ceremony.

DAY 26

All the citizens of Heliopolis came out to see the pharaoh and his young son, who looks like he is no more than four years old. I waited a long time until the two of them finally paraded through the main square. The pharaoh wore brightly colored robes. He looks very different from the way he looks in my drawing. I was expecting a tall, godlike creature, not even human. But he looks much like a regular man. I will draw him again.

Today is the big day and a very joyous occasion for all of Heliopolis. We are going to stand up the obelisk near the Temple of the Sun. Omari instructed me to bring papyrus and draw pictures so future generations of Egyptians will see how it was done. I will do as he says, but I still refuse to believe we will be successful. It looks like an impossible job. The obelisk is too large and heavy to stand up.

It appears that every able-bodied man in the surrounding area has been summoned to the Temple of the Sun.

Thick ropes have been attached to all sides of the obelisk.

The men have been gathered at the top of the sand hill. Pharaoh was hoisted up so he could stand on the obelisk. All of our eyes were on him.

"Pull!" the pharaoh shouted. "Pull!"

While the men pulled on the ropes with all their might, I drew a picture....

Hundreds of men pulled Cleopatra's Needle up the sand hill.

I could see their glistening sweat and hear their groans as they strained at the ropes. Very slowly, the sled that the obelisk lay upon began to slide up the slope of the hill. When the bottom of the obelisk reached the top of the hill, the men were ordered to stop pulling. Each of them was then given a shovel.

"Now dig!" shouted the pharaoh.

The men dug their shovels into the sand and dirt around the bottom of the obelisk. And slowly, almost by magic it seemed, the bottom of the obelisk began to sink into the sand as the top of the obelisk tilted upward.

"Keep digging!" shouted the pharaoh as the

obelisk continued to tilt upward. They were digging a hole in the top of the hill for the bottom of the obelisk to gently slide into.

When the obelisk was somewhat tilted, the men were told to stop digging. They were then divided into five large groups. Four of the groups were moved to the side near the bottom part of the obelisk. One of the groups was positioned on the side close to the top of the obelisk. The pharaoh was helped down from the obelisk.

He is a very smart man. Upon his order, workers brought his young son to the top of the obelisk and tied him to it with ropes. I asked a woman next to me why they were doing this. She told me that tying the pharaoh's son to the obelisk will ensure that the workers will be very careful when they pull it to its upright position. If they make a mistake and the obelisk topples over, it will break and the pharaoh's son will die.

That would be very sad. But the woman next to me said that it would not be too sad, because the pharaoh has one hundred sons.

Each of the five groups of men was ordered to take hold of a thick rope coming off the obelisk. Four of the groups were told they would pull the obelisk until it was upright. The other group was told to hold their rope tightly to make sure the obelisk did not get pulled too far upright and topple over.

"Go!" the pharaoh shouted.

The pharaoh's son is very brave. He only screamed and cried a little. I suppose he is used to helping his father in this way.

As the men pulled and strained at the ropes, I drew this picture....

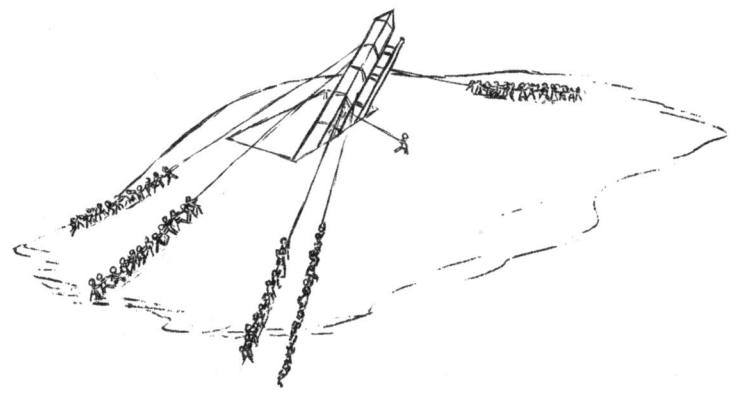

They dug a hole at the top of the hill for the obelisk to slide into.

I could not believe my eyes. The strength of hundreds of men—motivated by the pharaoh and the fear of killing his son—was somehow overcoming the weight of the obelisk. It was tilting upward.

"More!" the pharaoh shouted. "Harder!"

The obelisk continued tilting upward. When it was standing fully upright on its flat base, the men were ordered to stop pulling on the ropes. There were deafening cheers and congratulations from the people all around. The obelisk, for the first time, stood up on its own.

Somebody yelled, "It looks like a needle pointing up to the sun!"

DAY 27

After the obelisk was successfully raised, the workers were given shovels again and ordered to remove the dirt and sand that had been used to stand it up. Then they leveled the ground so you would never even know the hill had been there.

We went home and had a feast. My aunts and uncles and cousins were congratulating me on the drawings I made for the sides of the obelisk. Mother said that even though drawing pictures is not something one can do to earn a living, she is very proud of me. I was happy.

We had almost finished our meal when there was a knock at the door. It was Omari.

"Before he returns to Cairo," he told me, "the pharaoh wishes to meet you."

"Me?" I asked, disbelieving. "The pharaoh wants to meet me? There must be some mistake."

"We do not make mistakes. The pharaoh wishes to meet you, right away. Come with me, Lateef."

This time my mother did not fall to her knees. She beamed with pride.

"What will I say to the pharaoh?" I asked Omari as he led me through the busy streets. "I am afraid."

"You will say nothing," he replied. "You will listen."

Omari brought me to the grand palace in the center of the town. He led me inside, through huge golden doors. I had never been in the palace before. Only the wealthy and powerful are permitted inside. It is a beautiful place, with tiled floors, fine curtains, and heroic statues everywhere.

I was led into a room. And there, sitting before me on a gigantic throne, was the great Thutmosis III.

I could not believe I was in the same room as the pharaoh. I trembled in his presence and fell to my knees.

"The son of Ra, the son of the sun," I blubbered uncontrollably, "the King of Upper and Lower Egypt, the powerful and glorious—"

"Quiet!" spoke the pharaoh. "Stand up, Lateef."

I stopped blubbering and stood up. My name had passed through the pharaoh's lips.

"I have been informed that you are the artist who drew the hieroglyphs for the sides of my obelisk," spoke the pharaoh.

I could not move my mouth. I could only nod my head. Perhaps he did not like my work. Perhaps I was to be executed.

"You are a talented young man, Lateef," the pharaoh told me. He placed one hand on my shoulder. I almost fainted.

"Continue to work and improve your drawing," the pharaoh continued. "Someday when you grow up, you will come to Cairo and become my personal artist."

DAY 31

I still cannot believe it all happened. Every day I walk past the obelisk and gaze upon it, standing so tall and proud in front of the Temple of the Sun.

It seems a miracle that this glorious monument

to the pharaoh was carved out of raw granite that was once buried in the ground at Aswan. It seems a miracle that the strong men of Heliopolis were able to raise it up to point at the sun, Ra. And it seems a miracle that my drawings are now carved into the four sides of the obelisk.

Now the memory of Thutmosis III will live forever. My drawings will live forever. And the obelisk will stand proudly in Heliopolis for eternity.

MEANWHILE, IN THE PRESENT DAY...

Man, I bet my mom made that whole story up. How would *she* know how they stood the obelisk up in ancient Egypt? And how would she know that some kid drew the pictures that were carved into it? I really doubt the Egyptians wrote any of that stuff down.

"I thought those hieroglyphics were some kind of secret wise sayings," I said as I gazed at the faded symbols on the obelisk.

"You thought wrong," Mom replied as she got up from the bench. "They were just the pharaoh bragging about himself. Well, it's getting late. I guess we should start heading home."

"Before we go," I said, "one quick question. They didn't have trucks and cranes and stuff like that in ancient Egypt. If this thing weighs over two hundred tons, how did it get to America?"

"Oh, that's a long story," Mom replied. "You'd probably be bored. And I don't want you to miss your game."

"Give me the short version."

Mom explained that after they raised up the obelisk in Heliopolis, it stayed there for a *long* time—about 1,500 years. But during that time Egypt declined as a world power. It became part of the Roman Empire. Mom told me that in 12 BCE, Emperor Augustus Caesar had the obelisk moved to Alexandria, which is not far from Heliopolis. He raised it in front of the Caesarium, a temple honoring his father, Julius Caesar.

"Yeah, but how did it get to New York City?" I asked.

"Well," Mom said, "when the Roman Empire collapsed in western Europe between 395 AD and 476—"

"No, I don't want to hear that boring history stuff," I said to my mother. "Tell the story the way you told the first two."

"Okay, if you insist...."

PART 3

I AM A SPY.
THIS IS MY STORY.

(1879–1880)

Diary of Panya Hassan, a girl in Alexandria, Egypt, who witnessed Cleopatra's Needle being taken away from Egypt
Translated from Arabic

NOVEMBER 4, 1879

Today is my fourteenth birthday, so happy birthday to ME. Father called me into his room this morning and told me he wanted to give me a special gift. He handed me a book and said, "Panya, this is the greatest book I ever read."

I opened the book and was surprised to find that all the pages were BLANK! No words. No pictures. I thought he was playing a joke on me.

Father smiled and said someday this WILL BE the greatest book he ever read—after I write it. That is the book I am writing these words in now. Perhaps someday, someone will read it.

Father said he gave me this book because I am a very opinionated young lady, which I must admit is true. My name Panya means "mouse," but I am ANYTHING but a mouse. I care deeply about things, and I am not ashamed to express my feelings. But father says that sometimes I get angry and lash out at people, which is true, I suppose. I still did not understand why he gave me this book.

Then he started talking about locomotives. Father explained that in a locomotive, water is heated in a boiler. That creates steam in the engine, which makes the locomotive move forward. But if it gets TOO hot and there is TOO much steam, the boiler can explode. So the engineer will open something they call a "blow-off valve" to release some of the steam and ease the pressure on the engine.

"What does that have to do with me?" I asked.

Father said that when I am angry I become full of pent-up emotion, the same way the boiler on a locomotive becomes full of steam. He said that instead of acting out my anger, I should write my thoughts down in this book. That way I will have the chance to think things over before I lash out with words or actions. He said writing in this book could be my way to blow off steam.

I think father is a very smart man and I will follow his advice, even if he did compare me to a locomotive.

NOVEMBER 5, 1879

A group of Americans were at the Alexandria port today. All men. I had never seen an American before. They look like regular people, except they wear strange clothes and silly hats.

They are probably tourists. Americans are fascinated by Egypt. I suppose it is because the United States is a young nation, barely a hundred years old. Egypt has been around for THOUSANDS of years. Tourists want to come and see our pyramids and our Sphinx near Cairo. They want to witness the ancient world with their own eyes, as if they can't believe these things truly exist.

With my own eyes, I look upon these American men with distrust. They must have wives and families. Why would they come here and leave them at home? What are they doing in Egypt?

NOVEMBER 6, 1879

There are rumors swirling around about the Americans I saw yesterday. Some of my schoolmates say the Americans are planning to build a canal in Panama. So they want to examine our beautiful Suez Canal, which opened ten years ago. But it would take two days to walk to Suez from here, so why are they spending so much time in Alexandria?

Others say the Americans are searching for the

tomb of King Tutankhamun. He took the throne when he was just a boy and ruled Egypt from 1332 to 1323 BCE. Tutankhamun died when he was not even twenty years old. Many archeologists have searched for his tomb, but so far it has not been found.

Still others say the Americans are here to steal our treasures. The tourists come to see statues and artifacts of the ancient world. Then they take

Cleopatra's Needle in Alexandria, Egypt, 1879.

them home and put them in their private collections, or in museums. I believe we should keep our treasures in Egypt. If foreigners want treasures so badly, they should create their own.

NOVEMBER 7, 1879

Finally I discovered the true reason why the Americans have come to Egypt. Yes, they want to steal something. But apparently it is something none of us had even considered—Cleopatra's Needle! The grand obelisk has been standing on the shore here for many centuries, since 12 BCE. My friends just call it "Cleo."

During the Roman Empire, Cleo was brought to Alexandria and placed at the entrance to a temple honoring Julius Caesar. Cleopatra had built the temple, so people started calling it Cleopatra's Needle even though she had died long before the obelisk arrived. The temple is long gone, like so many treasures from the ancient world.

I am heartbroken and angry. Cleo is part of Alexandria, greeting ships in the harbor from near and far. The Americans want to steal one of our landmarks. It was stated as such in the newspaper, so it is now official. The rumor is that the

Americans are going to bring Cleo to Washington, Philadelphia, or New York City.

NOVEMBER 8, 1879

The situation with Cleo is even worse than I thought. The Americans are NOT stealing it. We are GIVING it to them! I can hardly believe I just wrote those words, or that they are true. I am FURIOUS.

Father told me he has been expecting this to happen ever since June, when Ismail Pasha, the khedive of Egypt, abdicated the throne and his son Mehmet Tewfik Pasha became the new khedive. Before he left, Khedive Ismail made an agreement with the Americans allowing them to remove Cleo and take it to the United States.

Why would he DO such a thing? We are all asking ourselves that question. It has to be money. That is what I think. Khedive Ismail spent a fortune building the Suez Canal and other projects. I know this because I read the newspaper. That is why I am smart.

Our nation's crops are failing this year, so there is little grain to sell to other nations. As a result, our government cannot pay its debts. I bet that Khedive Ismail told the Americans they could have Cleo because that will increase trade and tourism with the United States.

The old saying goes that the love of money is the root of all evil, and I believe that to be true. This is a sad day for Egypt. A sad day for the WORLD.

Khedive Ismail, ruler of Egypt.

NOVEMBER 10, 1879

Father told me that Americans have been snooping around Cleo for a long time. Twelve years ago, when I was a baby, a book writer named Mark Twain visited Alexandria. And just last February the former American President Ulysses S. Grant was here. I thought he was just a tourist seeing the sights. Perhaps President Grant had ANOTHER reason to be here. Perhaps he was sent here to convince Khedive Ismail to give up Cleo.

Americans cannot be trusted. When they want something, they just take it. That is how they formed their country, after all. Native people lived where the United States is today, and the Americans took their land away. The only difference here is that our government is actually GIVING the Americans our obelisk. How foolish people in power can be.

NOVEMBER 12, 1879

This will not be the first time another nation has come to Egypt and left with an obelisk as a souvenir. France took one of our obelisks in 1833. Just two years ago, England took another one. We only have a small number of obelisks in all of

Egypt. What will we have left to give to foreigners when all of our obelisks are gone?

The good news is that most people believe the Americans are going to fail in their mission. Men are even betting on it in the streets. I agree that the Americans will fail. You don't just pick up an obelisk and put it in your pocket. Cleo weighs many tons. It will not be easy to move. It took the French twenty-five years before they moved their obelisk to Paris. It took the British SEVENTY-FIVE years to move their obelisk to London. Six Englishmen drowned while they were moving it.

And that was just to sail the obelisk across the Mediterranean Sea. The Americans will have to move Cleo all the way across the Atlantic OCEAN. It will probably take them a hundred years, if they can do it at all. I say it is an impossible task. It cannot be done. Shame on anyone who tries.

NOVEMBER 14, 1879

I cried today. The American flag was raised atop Cleo. They have claimed it. It belongs to them now.

Father says this is partly our own fault, and he may be right. The obelisk is at the edge of Alexandria, near the Ramleh railway depot. That is a

When they put the American flag up, we knew we had lost Cleopatra's Needle.

bad part of town. Our citizens have not paid attention to Cleo or taken care of it. We neglected it. It seems so lonely standing there by itself.

Over the years, bad men have come with sledgehammers and broken off pieces of Cleo to sell to relic hunters. That is why the bottom corners are no longer sharp edges like they once were. Worse, I have seen thoughtless men stand at the obelisk and relieve themselves on it. They use it as a BATHROOM! There are disagreeable odors there. Many people do not want to go near Cleo. No wonder our government was willing to let the Americans take it.

"Egypt has other obelisks, Panya," Father told me.

I have not seen other obelisks myself. But it doesn't matter how many we have. Cleo is OUR monument. I say if the Americans like monuments so much, they should build their OWN. It is wrong to give away our monuments. In fact, I believe we should demand the return of ALL the treasures that have been stolen from us in the past by foreign nations.

Father refuses to do anything about it. He says it would be dangerous to resist the Americans, and our own government. He will not put his life on the line for a piece of stone. He says, "Calm down, Panya. Relax."

Well, I WON'T relax. I want to SCREAM! Father

may not be willing to do anything, but I am. We should fight back. I will not be a mouse.

NOVEMBER 15, 1879

I saw a poster on a bulletin board near the railway station yesterday. It announced a meeting of the Young Egyptian Party. I will paste it in this book....

STOP THE THEFT OF CLEOPATRA'S NEEDLE!

So many of our antiquities have been looted, stolen, damaged, and put on display in museums around the world. Do not let them steal another one!

People are starving in our country. Our nation is in debt.

We will fight back. That is what we will do. We will stop this. If our government will not stop the Americans, we will do it ourselves.

COME JOIN US!

I told Father I was going to meet a friend after school today, but the truth is I went to the meeting of the Young Egyptian Party. It was held in the back of a warehouse. When I walked inside, everyone looked at me. I realized I was the only girl there. That made me angry too. ALL Egyptians should do what they can to prevent the Americans from taking Cleo away.

I signed a paper that says I am a member of the Party. Somebody asked me what I am willing to do to help the cause. I said, "ANYTHING."

The older boys said they were afraid to put a girl in harm's way. Some of them did not even want me around. But somebody suggested that I could spy on the Americans, who would not suspect a young girl. Fine. I agreed to watch what the Americans do and report my findings back to the Young Egyptian Party. I will be good at spying, as I am an excellent observer.

NOVEMBER 18, 1879

I am starting to see articles in the newspaper about what the Americans intend to do with Cleo. Apparently, they have decided they are going to bring it to New York City and place it in a large park called Central. A man named Gorringe, who is a commander in the United States Navy, has been put in charge of removing the obelisk and bringing it to America.

Suddenly my fellow Egyptians are starting to take notice. There are other meetings like ours being held, petitions being passed around, and calls for action. Where were all these outraged citizens a year ago? Or five years ago, when it could have made a difference? Even today, many people, like my father, do not care if Cleo stays or goes. People only care about their jobs, or the price of bread.

There is a lesson to be learned here. We must appreciate the things that are meaningful to us, or they could be taken away.

NOVEMBER 21, 1879

I went to spy on the Americans today. I pretended to be a silly girl who has nothing better to do after school. They did not suspect me.

It looks like the Americans are moving fast to remove Cleo. Maybe they are afraid our government might change its mind and tell them to go home. That Gorringe man has hired at least one hundred Egyptian workers by my count. I watched as they started to clear the area around Cleo with shovels and rakes. Some of them look to be boys younger than me, and others are old men who can barely walk. No women or girls, of course. I suppose the Americans do not consider us capable of doing physical labor, just as Egyptians do not consider us capable of fighting back.

I watched as some of the workers dug with shovels around the obelisk. The older ones filled baskets with dirt. The younger ones carried the baskets to the shore and dumped the dirt in the water. I wrote down my observations and reported them to the Young Egyptian Party. I was thanked for my efforts, but I felt it was not enough. Just watching will not stop the Americans.

"What did you do after school today, Panya?" Father asked when I got home. I lied. I told him I was doing schoolwork. I feel bad about lying, but I feel good about what I am doing for my country.

NOVEMBER 22. 1879

More spying today. I observed that Gorringe man for the first time—the American in charge of moving Cleo. He is hard to miss. He is a tall man, over six feet. He has blue eyes, bluer than I have ever seen. Gorringe directs the workers, with the help of an Egyptian translator. From the moment I set my eyes on him, I DESPISED this man Gorringe.

I do not know how much Gorringe and the

Henry Gorringe.

Americans are paying these foolish Egyptians to help them. They work day and night. But today everything stopped for a moment when a stooped-over worker digging with a shovel unearthed some bronze amulets and other ancient objects. The Americans took possession of them and gave the man a few coins as a reward for his discovery. He seemed happy to take their money. IDIOT!

Before I left for the day, a group of protesters arrived. They yelled at the workers to stop helping the Americans. It did no good, of course. But I will say this. The workers do not appear to be in any rush to complete the job for the Americans. They work slowly. They say "the more days, the more dollars."

All they care about is money in their pockets. They don't care about Egypt losing our history. As long as they get paid. People will do ANYTHING for money. That is all we will have left after foreigners take away our treasures.

When they are not shoveling, I see some of the workers drinking alcohol, gambling, or fighting with one another. Then they stagger back to work looking sleepy. They are a DISGRACE to Egypt. They should be ASHAMED of themselves. I am DISGUSTED by them.

NOVEMBER 24, 1879

The area around Cleo has been cleared of dirt, garbage, and rubble. Now I can see the steps and the pedestal below the obelisk, which had been covered up my entire life. It looks lovely. If only the Americans were making Cleo look beautiful for OUR benefit. No, they only cleaned it up so it will be easier for them to take it away.

NOVEMBER 25, 1879

Today the workers built wooden scaffolding all around Cleo. After the scaffolding was up, I observed them putting wooden planking on all four sides of the obelisk. They must be covering it with wood to protect it during its long voyage to America.

I wonder where the Americans got so much wood. We have plenty of stone and granite in Egypt, but wood is a scarce resource. Maybe they brought the wood over from America. I hear they have plenty of it there. We have stone treasures. They have wood. They should build wooden treasures and leave our stone ones alone.

I fear the Young Egyptian Party must act soon or it will be too late. The Americans are bold. I have

Getting ready to take Cleo away.

seen them walking down the street and eating in our cafes. My fellow Egyptians hiss, curse, and threaten them as they walk by, but it doesn't seem to bother them. I wonder if they are even capable of feeling guilt or shame. Maybe they don't even know what they are doing is wrong.

NOVEMBER 27, 1879

I attended a meeting of the Young Egyptian Party today after school. Everyone is wondering how the Americans plan to bring Cleo across the Atlantic Ocean. It seems impossible. But Americans are clever. They must have a plan. There are only three options that we can see:

1. They could slide Cleo onto the deck of a ship. But the weight of the obelisk on even a very large vessel would make it top-heavy and unstable. It would easily capsize in bad weather.
2. They could attach the obelisk to the BOTTOM of a ship with ropes or chains. But then there is the risk of the chains breaking and losing the obelisk. Or it might bump into something under the water.
3. They could put it on a separate boat and TOW it to America. That is what the British did when they took their obelisk. But six of their men drowned in a storm and they

nearly lost the obelisk too. And that was just towing it across the Mediterranean Sea. The Americans will have to tow Cleo all the way across the ocean. Much more dangerous.

Whatever option the Americans choose, I believe they will fail. Cleo will most likely sink—like the stone that it is—into the sea. And then NOBODY will own it. It is a fool's mission.

During our group discussion, I reported what I have observed so far. Then we talked about our plan of action. There was a heated argument about the use of violence. Some members believe the only way to stop the Americans from taking Cleo will be to fight back, with weapons if necessary. One boy suggested it would be smarter to sabotage their efforts—poison their food or something like that. Others said they reject violence entirely, or they are only willing to use it in self-defense.

I am conflicted about this issue. I am not a mouse, and I want to fight back. But I am not an idiot.

Before we adjourned our meeting, a history student at the university stood up. He pointed out that the obelisk did not come from Alexandria originally, so we have no right to claim ownership of it. Many people did not know that Cleo was carved far to the south, in the granite quarries of Aswan. He informed them that the obelisk stood in Heliopolis for many centuries. It was brought to Alexandria by Caesar Augustus when the Roman Empire ruled our land. I knew all these things, because I read.

Another student said we have every right to keep Cleo because Aswan and Heliopolis are parts of Egypt. We didn't take the obelisk from another country, the way the Americans are doing. Someone else said that didn't matter because Egypt was not a formal country in ancient times.

These are complicated issues that I don't fully understand. I do not know if violence is justified. I only know that I am angry. I feel in my heart that it is not right for foreigners to come here and take things that do not belong to them, even if our government has given them permission to do so. But I am not certain the will of our people is to risk their lives to keep Cleo in Alexandria.

NOVEMBER 29, 1879

On my spy mission today I saw teams of divers swimming in the waters near the shore where Cleo stands. I went snooping around to find out what they were up to. I discovered the divers were hired by that Gorringe man.

One of the workers told me the waters around Alexandria are littered with large chunks of ancient temples and Roman ruins that were discarded centuries ago. The Americans are worried that when they remove Cleo, their boat might bump against the debris below the waterline. Some of it even sticks up from the sea. So they are removing it in preparation for taking Cleo away.

We are running out of time.

NOVEMBER 30, 1879

No school today. We held another meeting this morning. The big question is how will this Gorringe man lower Cleo to the ground safely in order to take it away? He cannot simply push it over onto its side. The obelisk would break in two.

Then I learned the answer to that question.

When I arrived at my usual spot to spy on the Americans, suspicious activity was going on. A bunch of large carts were on the site. Gorringe and his men were unpacking crates, which were full of iron parts and wood. The Americans are building something.

I watched as Gorringe and the workers put the pieces together. They assembled two identical towers and placed them on either side of Cleo. Gradually, it became obvious that Gorringe is building some kind of device that will be attached to the obelisk and swivel it from the vertical to a horizontal position. A TURNING MACHINE. After the obelisk has been turned on its side, the Americans will lower it to the ground, drag it to the shore, and put it on their boat.

Several of us saw what the Americans are up to, and an emergency meeting of the Young Egyptian Party was called. For many minutes I sat as the leaders complained about the evil Americans. Finally, I stood up.

"The time for talk is over!" I shouted.

All eyes turned to me. Up until that moment I had been quiet during our meetings, letting others take the lead. But I could no longer hold my tongue.

"Any day now," I said, "the Americans are going to turn the obelisk with the machine they are building. Once they turn it, there will be nothing we can do. It will be too late. We must take action NOW!"

There was silence in the room.

"She is just a girl," somebody said. "What does she know?"

A few of the others muttered in agreement. But one boy stood up.

"Panya is right," he said. "We need to stop talking and DO something."

"We could dump more debris into the harbor," someone suggested. "It will rip a hole in the Americans' boat."

"What do we have to dump?" asked someone else.

"It will be too late by then, anyway," another man said.

Other suggestions were offered. One man suggested setting fire to the wooden turning mechanism. Somebody else said we should raise money and bribe the workers to stop helping the Americans.

The meeting ended with no firm plan, but there seemed to be agreement among everyone that we need to act, and to do something BEFORE Gorringe turns the obelisk. We are becoming more bold as we become more desperate.

DECEMBER 1, 1879

I told Father I was going to school, but I went to spy on the Americans instead. They are very clever, but I still believe they will fail. Their turning machine looks flimsy to me. Cleo weighs over two hundred TONS. The wooden machine they are building is sure to buckle under that much weight.

Even if they can successfully turn Cleo sideways, it will crack in half. I am sure of that. The weight on either side will be too great for their turning machine. I am afraid that innocent Egyptians will get hurt when the machine collapses. Cleo will fall and possibly land on people.

As the Americans were building their foolish machine, some other members of the Young

Egyptian Party joined me to watch and to curse their efforts.

"It is the work of the devil!" I shouted. I could not help myself.

Another member of our group shouted, "It is the work of the devil!" And then another. Soon we were all chanting, "It is the work of the devil! It is the work of the devil!" More people joined in.

The Americans saw and heard us, but they did not stop our protest. From what I understand, free speech is something Americans cherish, so they allowed us to continue chanting. But I have also heard that if anybody tries to take down the American flag from on top of Cleo, they will be shot.

DECEMBER 3, 1879

The turning machine seems to be completed, and the Americans removed the scaffolding around Cleo. Now they could turn it horizontal any time they want.

It is now or never. If nobody else is going to do anything, I decided, I will do something.

In the middle of the night, I crept silently out

of my bed and went to the workshop where Father keeps his tools. He has one handsaw he uses to cut large objects. I climbed on the stepladder and took the saw off the wall.

I put it in a cloth sack and made my way through the darkness to the banks of the Ramleh railway depot. I ran and walked, hiding in the shadows. It was less than a mile, but it felt like five. I was out of breath when I made it to Cleo.

There was nobody guarding it, just as I had hoped. I removed the saw from my sack and placed the blade against one of the wooden boards near the bottom of the turning machine. While spying on the Americans, I had determined that if one of those boards could be cut in two, the whole machine might collapse.

I began sawing the wood. The saw made some noise, but I tried to work as quietly as possible. I made it about halfway through the board. I just needed a few more minutes to cut all the way through.

"Hey!" somebody suddenly shouted in English. "You!"

I turned around. Two Americans were standing there with a lantern.

"It's a girl!" one of them yelled.

"Drop the saw!" ordered the other.

Both men had guns. They grabbed me and ripped the saw out of my hands.

"Come with us," they ordered.

They threw me in a large wagon pulled by a horse. I didn't know where they were taking me. Maybe they were going to put me in jail. Or worse. I begged for their mercy. They refused to speak to me the whole time we were in the wagon. I have never been so frightened in my life. We traveled a long time in the dark. Finally, we arrived at a house. My house.

"Is this where you live?" one of the Americans asked.

"Yes."

"Get out," the other one ordered. "Try that again and you will see what will happen to you. You are lucky you are just a child."

"Can I have my saw back?" I asked.

"No!"

Father was furious when he was awakened from his sleep. He was furious at me for sneaking out in the middle of the night. He was furious at me for taking his saw without permission and letting the Americans take it away. And he was furious at me for risking my life.

But at the same time, I noticed a little gleam in his eye when it was all over. I think he was secretly just a LITTLE proud of me for what I had attempted. I may have failed in my mission, but you also fail if you don't try.

DECEMBER 4, 1879

I was not going to go watch Gorringe and the Americans turn Cleo on its side today. I thought it would be too painful to see. But everybody else was going and Father didn't punish me, so I decided to go.

It looked like the whole town was there to bear witness to the sad event. When I got there, I could see that the Gorringe had replaced the board I had sawed halfway through. He also had a team of security guards in a big circle around Cleo to prevent troublemakers like me from disrupting things. There would be no stopping him now.

Before he could turn Cleo on its side, Gorringe

would have to raise it a few inches off its pedestal. To do this, he had a machine called a hydraulic jack. It used water to lift up heavy objects. I don't know how it worked, but it was like magic. We watched in amazement as the 220-ton obelisk was silently lifted straight up off its pedestal.

It looked like today was going to be a horrible day. But it turned out to be WONDERFUL. You see, Gorringe had forgotten about one important detail—the crabs!

I should explain. In Roman times, a bronze sculpture in the shape of a crab had been attached to the base below each of the four corners of Cleo to stabilize it. Why crabs? During the Roman Empire, crabs symbolized strength. The Romans even put images of crabs on their coins.

When Gorringe gave the signal for his men to pull on the cables to turn Cleo, the bottom of the obelisk bumped against the crabs and it did not move an inch! Perhaps Gorringe is not quite as clever as we thought he was.

We all cheered. I knew the Americans would fail! The gods are conspiring against them.

Now they will have to abandon this foolish endeavor. They will finally see their folly and go home. What a glorious day it was for Alexandria, and all of Egypt!

DECEMBER 5, 1879

The Americans did NOT give up and go home. They simply removed the crabs from the top of the pedestal. They are going to try again. I will say one thing about Gorringe. He is not a quitter.

All morning, rumors were spreading that there was going to be a big protest at Cleo today when the Americans again attempt to turn it. Hundreds of people are here. The crowd is noisy. Our beloved Cleo is attached to a complicated system of pulleys, winches, rope, and steel cables. On one side of the obelisk, a tall stack of wooden pallets has been positioned. I don't know what they are there for. The Americans are not using a steam engine to operate their turning machine, as far as I can tell.

It is 11 a.m. Everyone is watching with fear and sadness in their eyes.

Gorringe just shouted, "Go!"

Six men on one side of Cleo are pulling on the cables attached to the top. The crowd has fallen silent.

There is a creaking sound. Very slowly Cleo is beginning to turn.

The obelisk is starting to turn.

"It's moving!" somebody shouted.

Wait! There is a sudden loud SNAP, like the sound of a bullwhip. One of the steel guide wires has broken! I KNEW the Americans would fail! I prayed that their entire turning machine would collapse in a heap. It would serve them right.

Cleo stopped moving for a moment... and then it began moving FASTER.

It appeared to be out of control!

People began to scatter in all directions for fear that Cleo and the entire turning machine would fall on top of them. There was screaming.

But Gorringe did not panic.

"Slack the other cable!" he ordered calmly.

Cleo continued turning. When it reached the point of being horizontal, it banged against the stack of wooden pallets that had been placed below it. So THAT'S why the pallets were there—to cushion the fall.

Cleo bounced a foot or two and then settled back onto the stack of wood. The top two pallets were damaged, but the obelisk was horizontal. It had not broken. Nobody was hurt.

And then, suddenly, there were cheers. Not from me. I would not cheer for the Americans. But other people did. I guess they could not help themselves. It was an amazing accomplishment, I had to admit. It had seemed impossible to gently turn a two-hundred-ton piece of stone sideways, but the Americans figured out a way to do it. I must admit they are an ingenious people.

For the first time in nearly two thousand years, Cleo was not standing up straight and tall. It was lying on its side, as if asleep. Or dying.

Slowly, the crowd began to disperse and the American flag was repositioned. This is a sad day for Alexandria, and all of Egypt. I weep.

It was lying on its side, as if asleep. Or dying.

DECEMBER 6, 1879

I am so mad, and it has nothing to do with Cleo. I just found out that the beautiful statue of a lady holding a torch in the air was supposed to come to Egypt, but instead it will be going to the United States. NOT FAIR! What happened was that the Khedive hired a sculptor to make that grand statue to greet ships as they entered the Suez Canal. But our country ran out of money. So the sculptor sold it to France instead, and they are giving it to America as a gift. Why does the world give America so many gifts? What did the Americans ever do to deserve them?

MARCH 29, 1880

I apologize. I have not written in this book since December. I was too saddened by what happened to Cleo. Everyone was. Even Father. I believe he feels partly responsible for not doing anything to stop Gorringe and the Americans.

After they turned the obelisk sideways, I could not bear to go back and watch them take it away. But I did enjoy hearing about their struggle.

It took them WEEKS just to drag Cleo down a short ramp. And they still have to move it miles to the port, where the water is deep enough for big ships to dock. Who knows how long will it take them to bring it to New York City?

The proud merchants of Alexandria refused to give Gorringe permission to move Cleo over the city streets. They claimed that the weight would damage the pipes that carry water under the streets. That is probably not true, but good for them. I approve of anything that will make it harder for the Americans to take Cleo away.

Gorringe and his troublemakers have spent the last few months building a huge watertight container, which they will use to tow the obelisk to the harbor. They also took apart their turning machine so they can ship it to New York City and use it to turn Cleo upright again.

Now there is NOTHING at the site where Cleo stood so proudly for so long.

MARCH 31, 1880

It all ended this morning. The Americans have left us, and they took Cleo with them. They will tow it to Alexandria harbor and load it onto a larger boat. From there, they will take it to America.

To me, this is like taking a child away from their mother. Many of us gathered at the shore to wave goodbye, with tears in our eyes.

I still believe Gorringe will fail. He has only completed the easy part. He still has to get the obelisk onto a boat, then sail it across the ocean. And March is the stormy season. With a little bit of luck—BAD LUCK—he will encounter a hurricane or an iceberg on the way to America.

Now that it is gone, people are saying they hope Cleo slips into the ocean and stays there for eternity. If we cannot own it, nobody should own it. Even the clever Americans would not be able to pull it up from the bottom of the sea.

In any case, it is out of our hands. There is nothing we can do.

Well, there is ONE thing I can do. And I have done it. I put a curse on this Gorringe man. Misfortune will come to him. It may not be today and it may not be tomorrow, but it will come. Mark my words.

Goodbye, Cleo.

MEANWHILE, IN THE PRESENT DAY...

Mom sighed as she picked up her purse from the bench.

"It looks like we missed our train," she said. "But there's another one in twenty minutes. I think we can make it if we hurry...."

"Wait a minute!" I said. "Did you make all that stuff up? Do you expect me to believe that people used to pee on Cleopatra's Needle when it was in Egypt? And that they *gave* it to us as a present? For *free*? Weren't ships a lot smaller back in those days? How did they find one big enough to hold this thing? And how did they get the obelisk onto a ship anyway?"

"You're certainly very curious all of a sudden," Mom said as she put her hand on my forehead the way she does when I'm sick. "Are you feeling okay?"

"Just go on," I told her. "How did they get it across the Atlantic Ocean? I don't care if we miss the train."

"Well..."

PART 4

I AM A STOWAWAY.
THIS IS MY STORY.

(1880)

*Diary of Thomas Brighton, a boy on the ship that brought
Cleopatra's Needle to America*

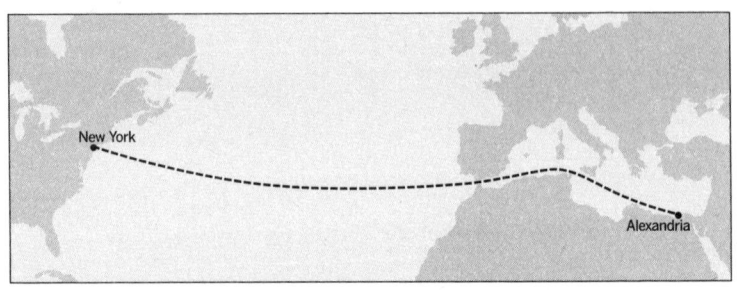

The route from Egypt to New York City.

APRIL 4, 1880

I must start this diary by saying I am sorry in advance for my bad speling. I never went to school or had a teacher to help me learn. But I am trying to get better by myself. The more I practice the better I will become. So I will ~~right rite~~ write in this diary every day until someday I will be able to write and spell the ~~write rite~~ right way. I must go for now, but tomorrow is another day.

APRIL 5, 1880

Why am I doing this? You are probably asking. I am doing this so that if I die someone might see these words & maybe remember me in some small way. They will remember that I lived & my life mattered. Every human beings life should have meaning. Even mine. I am somebody.

But I don't even know how old I am. I am not sure, anyway. People say I look like I am about 10 years old. But I could be as young as 8 or as old as 12. I can't say for sure because I have no berth certificate. I don't know when my birthday is. I have never had a birthday party, that I remember. I have no address. I have no parents.

Not anymore, anyway. I once had parents, of course. My mother worked in a bake shop, but I barely remember her. My father was a mechanic. He could fix anything. We lived in England then, north of London. Instead of sending me to school, I was my father's helper in the factory from the time I was very little. He taught me how the machines worked, & how to fix them when they broke down. I liked doing that, & I got good at it. But that was a wile ago. I have not seen either of my parents in years.

Mother & father yelled at each other allot. They also drank ~~too much~~ allot. Sometimes there was hitting. I don't want to think about it anymore. But that is when I ran away. & I do not regret it for a minute, despite all that has happened to me since then.

I made my way to London on a bus, but there

was nothing for me there so I kept going south. My parents tried to find me & bring me home. They almost succeeded. But I managed to avoid them, & the police.

They were chasing me when I stowed away on a boat that got me across The English Channel to France. I will never go back to England again. I will never see my family again. & I don't care.

I did not speak French & could not be understood by the people there. So I kept moving. Sometimes on trains. Sometimes on foot. Sometimes people helped me with food or coins. Sometimes people were mean to me. Sometimes I went without eating four days at a time. This has not been an easy life. But I am alive. & that is all that matters.

I do not know exactly how I got to the city of Alexandria, which is in the northern part of Egypt. All I remember was that I was in Italy & some bad men were chasing me because I took some food off the table where they were eating. I thought they were finished eating, but I guess they weren't. It doesn't matter now. I hid out on the first boat I saw. & then it started moving. I didn't know where it was going.

It took me here, to Egypt, on the continent of Africa. I do not understand the language they speak here either. I must find a way to get out of this place. I cannot stay here, & I am not going back to England. There is nothing for me there, except for other people who speak the English language. I don't know where my life will lead me after this.

APRIL 14, 1880

Today I watched as an Egyptian family ate their dinner in a sidewalk restaurant on Fouad Street. Why do people order meals & not finish them? They waste so much good food. I eat every scrap of food I can get my hands on. When the family paid their bill & got up to leave, I ran over to the table before the busboy came to clear off their plates. I grabbed as much as I could carry in my hands, mouth, & pockets. It will be enough food to last me for a few days, at least. This is not stealing, I believe. The food would only be thrown in the garbage if I did not take it.

Alexandria is a big harbor city on the Mediterranean Sea about 200 kilometers from the capitol city, Cairo. There are lots of boats coming in & out all the time. Mostly small fishing boats. I spend my days watching boats in the harbor to see if one of them might be able to take me somewhere, anywhere. But I have no money to pay for a fare. I will need to sneak aboard a boat. This, I believe, is also not stealing. The boats are going to go where they go weather I am on them or not. It does not cost them anything for me to be on them, so why should I have to pay?

Someday I will have a job so I can earn money & buy my own food, boat rides, & other things I need. Until that day comes, I must do what I can to survive.

JUNE 7, 1880

It will be very hard for me to sneak aboard a small fishing boat. But I have been watching one particular black vessel in the harbor for several days now. The name on the side of it is Dessoug.

The Dessoug is the biggest steamer in the harbor & it has been sitting in the water ever since I got here. It is not in great shape. I can see that it is filthy & there is damage on the starboard side near the waterline. I thought that perhaps it had been abandoned.

But today I saw a group of very important looking men in nice clothes having serious discussions, walking around & pointing at parts of the ship. Before they left, they lowered the Egyptian flag & raised an American flag on the masthead. That was curious.

They were speaking English with American accents, which I don't hear a lot. I crept closer so I could make out what the men were saying without letting them know I was listening. It was good to hear my own language again.

I may be mistaken, but it sounded like the men in nice clothes have bought The Dessoug & plan to sail it to America. I do not know why.

I have never been to America. People say it is an amazing place where the streets are paved with gold. I don't believe a word of that. Gold is probably the worst material one could use to pave a street. But they say there is freedom in America. People can do & say & believe what they want there. & best of all, English is spoken in America.

America is the land of opportunity, they say. So that is where I hope to go. Perhaps I could go to America & start a new life there. But first I will have to find a way to get aboard The Dessoug.

JUNE 8, 1880

The strangest thing happened today. I observed a group of laborers with screwdrivers & other tools removing some of the plates on the hull of The Dessoug. I counted over 30 plates they took off, each one a few feet tall & wide. They took off thousands of rivets. They made a big hole in the side of the ship.

The boat is in dry dock & the hole is above the waterline. But even so, why would anyone cut a hole in the side of a ship? A ship needs to be watertight, of course.

As the day wore on, I could see that much work was going on inside the cargo hold of The Dessoug. Hammering & drilling & banging. Lots of activity. I could not tell what the men were doing in there. It looks like they are trying to strengthen the inside of the ship's hold with steel beams. They are getting The Dessoug ready for something. It appears as though they are trying to make the old wreck seaworthy.

I have come up with a plan. I will sneak into The Dessoug threw the hole they have opened up. Then I will not have to board the ship in the usual way & present a ticket. I could go to America, if in fact that is where The Dessoug will be going. But I will wait until the right moment, when I can sneak on without being seen.

JUNE 9, 1880

Now I know why they cut the hole in the side of The Dessoug. It is so they can put something inside the ship that is too big & heavy to put on the deck. The thing is completely covered by wooden boards, but it is the shape of an obelisk. I think they are going to slide it into the hole!

From what I have overheard on the street, a large obelisk stood near the shore here until recently. It had been there for centuries, ever since it was carved by ancient Egyptians.

And then the Americans came. I don't know how they did it, but they talked the Egyptian government into giving this obelisk to The United States. Or maybe they are just stealing it. But that is a pretty big thing to steal. Somebody would notice for sure.

Anyway, before they brought it to the harbor, the Americans had to lower the obelisk to the ground. That must have been a heckuva job! The thing is solid rock. How did they topple it over without breaking it? I will never know. But then last night, they rolled it here by putting it on top of cannonballs in an iron track.

Today as I was sitting here watching the ship, I saw a large group of men. There must have been

100 of them or more. & they were not fancy men in fancy clothes. They looked like laborers. Only a few of them were speaking English. They were using ropes & brute force to pull the obelisk along the dock until it was very close to The Dessoug.

I decided to join them. My hope was that the Americans might see me helping in their efforts & hear me speaking English. Perhaps they will invite me to be part of the crew when the ship sails. & if they don't, helping them might give me the opportunity to see the inside of the ship & find a hiding place on it.

It was very hard work, even for 100 of us. The obelisk is even heavier than it appears. But inch by inch, we dragged it over to the ship. One of the Americans seems to be in charge, telling everybody what to do. Nobody told me to leave. They need all the help they could get.

When the obelisk was almost touching The Dessoug, half of us were ordered to go around to the top of the obelisk & push it into the ship. I was using all my might. The men around me were grunting & sweating from the ~~aggzertion eggsertion~~ exertion. After hours of this, we pushed the obelisk into the cargo hold of The Dessoug.

They made a hole in the ship so they could
fit the obelisk inside!

I did not think the obelisk would fit inside. But it did, just barely & at a crooked angel. The obelisk takes up most of the ship's hold. After the job was done, we were ordered to wedge it in on both sides with planks of wood so it wouldn't slide back & forth when the ship moves.

The Dessoug is big. I could see there is room inside the hold for me to hide. Nobody has asked me to join the crew, so I guess I will have to sneak aboard. Maybe today.

This obelisk must be very special for the Americans to go threw all this trouble. But if they can bring this big rock to America, they can bring me to America with it.

JUNE 10, 1880

Two guards watch The Dessoug all day, so I had no chance to sneak aboard. Soon the Americans will replace the plates that were removed & close up the hole in the side of the ship. I will have to move fast.

I watched the men guarding The Dessoug all day. At sundown, one of them left his post. That left just one guard, a small man who had a gun at his side at all times. But he doesn't seem all that attentive, & I think he is a drinker. Even in the dark, I could see him remove something from his pocket, put it to his mouth, & tilt his head back.

I am hiding behind a wagon & watching him carefully as he walks back & forth in front of The Dessoug. He takes another drink, & another. He walks wobbly, mumbling something to himself. He is drunk. I am going to make my move as soon as he—

JUNE 11. 1880

I am aboard The Dessoug! I have nothing more than the clothes on my back, but I do not care. I am where I want to be—on a boat that will ~~beheading~~ be heading for The United States of America. I am so happy rite now. I will just have to hope they do not check the cargo hold for stowaways before we push off. I tried to sleep on the bed of pine wood across the bottom, but it is impossible. I am too excited, & scared.

JUNE 12. 1880

I was awakened by sunlight streaming thru the hole in The Dessoug. Then there was the sound of metal plates & banging. Workers riveted the plates back on. It didn't take long for them to fill in the hole. Nobody noticed me hiding in the cargo hold.

Now it is near total darkness in here. I know

my handwriting is even more crooked & hard to read than usual. I write these words by the faint light coming through a thin crack between two planks above my head.

It must have been around two o'clock in the afternoon when steam whistles were blown & we shoved off. I felt the boat creak, scrape against something, & then rock gently on the water. An engine rumbled to life, & then the propeller. I heard whistles & cheering, or maybe it was jeering, until it faded away into the distance.

I am finally on my way to America! I have heard stories about America. Stories of poor men who became rich, & rich men who lost everything they had. I guess that is why some games are called "games of chance." There is the chance you will win, & the chance you will lose. But in America, at least you get a chance.

JUNE 13, 1880

I wish I had taken more food with me. It has been a full day at sea now. I am not feeling well. The Atlantic is larger than I expected. I am getting hungry & thirsty. I don't know how long I can hold out. There is nothing to eat or drink down here.

Just a very big obelisk covered with wood, & some crates of stuff.

& a bucket, thank goodness. If not for this bucket, well, I would be in even worse shape. I am sure it smells pretty bad down here. But I don't notice it anymore. They say you get used to bad smells after a wile.

But the darkness is getting to me. I can barely see my hand in front of my face. I hope we get to America soon. Maybe we are going to New York City. I have always wanted to go there.

JUNE 15, 1880

This date is approximate. I do not know the exact date. I have lost track of night & day. I am so thirsty & weak I can barely sit up to write this. I must reveal myself or I am afraid that I will starve down here before we even get to America. I am going to bang on the ceiling. There is no other choice. These may be the last words I write.

JUNE 16, 1880

The men who pulled me out of the hold were angry. I was afraid they were going to throw me overboard. They speak many languages, & a few of them speak English. From what I understand, they were so angry because they have a very limited amount of food & water, & they don't want to share it with me.

They asked how I snuck onto the ship & I told them the truth. I begged them to let me live, & so far they have agreed. They gave me sips of water & a little food. I don't know what the food was, but I accepted it gratefully. It tasted like potato. When I get to America, I am determined to try a hot dog. I don't really want to eat dog, but apparently that is what people eat in America.

My leg is now chained to a pole so I cannot escape. Where do they think I will go? There is nothing but water as far as the eye can see. At least they did not take away my diary. The Americans have not decided what to do with me. I will try to act as young as possible, so maybe they will be kinder & take pity on me.

Despite everything, it is a pleasure to be up on deck & breathing fresh air.

JUNE 17, 1880

I have learned that we have not even reached the Atlantic Ocean yet! We are still in the

Mediterranean Sea. It seems as big as an ocean. We passed the island of Malta today. The waters are gentle & as I watch the clouds slide by in the sky, it looks like we are making good progress, about 7 knots per hour. I heard one of the men say "New York City," so I guess that's wear we are heading.

The man in charge seems to be an American who the men call "Commander Gorringe." Or at least I think he is in charge. When he tells the men to do something, they do it.

This Gorringe fellow has seen me. He knows I am here. We have not spoken yet. I believe he is trying to decide whether to keep me here or have me thrown overboard. I suppose he does not want to get to know me so that he can throw me overboard & not feel guilty about it. But I am determined to be very nice to him, & to all the crew, in order to win them over. I will help them any way I can. They can keep me alive.

I have noticed something very curious. Regardless of the language they speak, the men who work on this ship move their mouths even when they are not eating or speaking. I do not know why they do that.

JUNE 18, 1880

I figured out why the crewmen move their mouths even when they are not eating or speaking. They are chewing something they call "gum." You do not swallow it. You just chew it & spit it out at some point. The whole thing seems silly to me, but the men must get some enjoyment out of it.

We did not have gum in England when I was growing up there. But apparently it is a rubbery substance that has licorice or other flavoring. The crew call it "Black Jack." I asked one of the men if I could have a piece, & he took it out of his mouth and handed it to me. I chewed on it for a while, but it was utterly tasteless. I do not see the attraction.

JUNE 19, 1880

The Dessoug suddenly slowed down around noon today for no reason that I could see. Commander Gorringe gathered a group of crewmen around him & they disgust the situation. I could not hear their conversation, but I did hear the word "leak" repeatedly. Finally it became clear that there was a leak in the boiler that heats the water to power the engine.

I new why everyone was so worried. If the boiler fails, the ship stops dead. If you are stuck in open water for days, your food & water supplies will dwindle to nothing. Unless a rescue ship happens to come along, everyone onboard will die.

I was foolish to stowaway on this ship. I should have waited for another one. I could have stayed in Alexandria. I could have done so many things differently.

All the men looked worried, including Commander Gorringe.

"Let us pray," he said.

Commander Gorringe & the entire crew knelt down in prayer, and so did I. There was silence, except for the water slapping against the hull. I thought about the leak in the boiler & what could be done to repair it. I had worked on boilers with my father. Then I came up with an idea.

"Plug it with gum!" I shouted.

The men stopped there prayer. They turned around & looked at me.

"What did you say?" asked Commander Gorringe.

"Plug the hole in the boiler with your gum," I told him. "It will seal it up so you can continue on your way."

Commander Gorringe thought about what I had said for a moment. Then he ordered the men to take the gum out of their mouths & combine it into one large ball. He brought it over to me.

"Do you know how to plug a hole in a boiler?" he asked.

"I can try," I replied.

He unlocked the chain from my leg & took me to the engine room. The boiler was not the same as the boilers I had worked on with my father, but I figured all boilers work the same way. I stuffed the ball of gum into the hole, pushing the gum with my fingers until it filled the gap. I knew it would take a while for the gum to harden, but it appeared to have sealed up the hole. The engine roared to life.

"It works!" somebody said.

A few of the men clapped me on the back. When we had returned to full speed, Commander Gorringe smiled at me. Maybe he will let me stay alive for a while. Maybe he will throw somebody else overboard in my place. I resolved to make myself as useful as possible so he will allow me to live & get to New York City.

JUNE 23, 1880

I have not written here in several days because I have been very busy working on the ship. After 12 days at sea, we finally reached Gibraltar, which is at the lower tip of Spain & just miles from the north coast of Africa. The Dessoug is docking here for a few days so we can take on more coal—550 tons of it. & I feel like I shoveled it all myself.

Some fancy pants politicians & their wives came aboard to take a peek at the obelisk by candlelight. They were disappointed that it was covered with wood. But Mr. Gorringe refused to remove it for them.

He could have kicked me off the ship here in Gibraltar. Then he would not have to feed me anymore. He could have had me sent back to England. But he sees that I am a hard worker & has decided to let me stay onboard. He is a good man. I was given some clean clothes to wear & even a cot to sleep in.

At the end of the day, me & a bunch of the crewmen jumped into the water. I had not had a bath in weeks. It felt like heaven.

JUNE 26. 1880

After three days of working to get The Dessoug shipshape, we left Gibraltar around midnight. From here, it will be a straight shot to America. They say it is about 5,800 kilometers, or as the Americans would say, 3,600 miles. If we have no big problems, we should reach New York City sometime next month. I will get a hot dog then.

The sea is smooth. The winds are fair. We are unlikely to bump into icebergs during the summer months, so there should be no problems. But I never trust the weather.

JULY 1. 1880

We passed the Azores, a group of small islands in the Atlantic. We did not stop. Commander Gorringe wants to get to New York as quickly as possible. He said he needs to get the obelisk to Central Park before winter sets in & it might be too cold for the men to work outside.

I am not getting paid, but everyone is treating me like I am a member of the crew now. The other men seem to enjoy my company, even though we don't speak the same language. Today I showed them how to juggle, something I learned to do when I was in France. Juggling is a fairly simple skill, but the men seem to think it is amazing for a human being to keep 3 balls in the air at once. They kept shaking their heads & saying, "3 balls. 2 hands. How?" Many of them wanted to try it, & there was much laughter when the balls went flying all over the place.

I have been working hard too, shoveling coal, swabbing the deck, & doing other chores. So I have had little time to rite here. We are still more than 3,000 kilometers, I mean 1,800 miles, from America.

JULY 6. 1880

Disaster. At 2 o'clock this afternoon there was a sudden BANG & the engines stopped. Once again, we were dead in the water. Maybe this ship is cursed. Maybe I should have gotten off in Gibraltar, when I had the chance.

As soon as it happened, everybody looked at me. Even Commander Gorringe.

"What are you looking at me for?" I asked.

"You are the fixer," one of the crew said.

We went to the engine room to see what the problem was. At first I thought the boiler had broken & I would be blamed for it. But it wasn't the boiler. It was the crankshaft, which is a long metal rod that connects the engine to the propellers. It had broken in 2.

The other men seem to think that I am a wizard mechanic, which I am not. True, I am pretty good at fixing things that break, but I cannot repair a shattered crankshaft. Astonishingly (that is a big word) Commander Gorringe found a spare crankshaft in storage.

"Can you install it, Thomas?" he asked me.

"I'll try."

I had never seen a crankshaft before. I didn't even know what a crankshaft was. But I looked the broken one over, & it seemed pretty obvious how to remove it and install the new one. It would not be easy work. We would be floating in the middle of the Atlantic for a few days, at least.

Commander Gorringe ordered the sails up so we could catch some wind. But the sails don't do much. I don't know how the old time explorers from Europe made it across the ocean without steam engines & propellers.

JULY 9. 1880

Another situation came up today. While we were floating there and I was working on the crankshaft, one of the crew spotted something in the distance. It was a ship, & it was steaming directly toward us at great speed.

"High alert!" shouted Commander Gorringe.

He ordered everyone to hide anything of value. I don't have anything of value (well, maybe this diary), but I knew what he was worried about. The men on the other ship could be pirates. If they found out about the obelisk below our deck, they might try take over the Dessoug, rob us, or worse—execute us. I was afraid, & again deeply regretted not getting off in Gibraltar.

Everybody started rushing around franticly. As the other ship got closer, our crew huddled together.

"Be calm," Commander Gorringe told us as the ship pulled alongside ours. "Do not do anything to provoke them."

An officer climbed out on the deck of the other ship.

"Are you in distress?" he hollered threw a megaphone. "Do you need assistance?"

We all let out a breath of relief. It wasn't pirates. The ship was an Austrian fishing vessel.

"We can offer you bread & water," the officer shouted. "& fish, of course."

Commander Gorringe accepted some loaves of bread & tried to pay for them, but the Austrian officer refused to accept any money. He explained that it was maritime law to help a ship in distress. We all thanked him & his crew, & waved as they went on their way.

JULY 10, 1880

It had taken me a few days, but I removed the broken crankshaft & replaced it with the new one. I gave the news to Commander Gorringe.

"Okay, let's give her a go," he ordered.

The engines were turned on & the propellers began to spin. A cheer went up from the crew. They all clapped me on the back & sang a song about me being a jolly good fellow. That felt good.

Once again we are on our way & heading for New York. It is smooth sailing & I was able to take a much needed rest.

In talking with the other English speaking men on the crew, I now have some information about the obelisk we are carrying below deck. They told me it was carved out of granite in Egypt many centuries ago & brought to Alexandria by Augustus Caesar. The Americans did not steal it. The Egyptians gave it to them.

The rumor is that Egypt was going broke & gave the Americans the obelisk as a gift so tourists would come to Egypt & spend their money to see Egypt's other treasures, including the pyramids. I don't know if that is true. But I can't think of any other reason why they would give up such a treasured object. They say the Egyptian government even sold The Dessoug to Commander Gorringe. That's how badly they needed money. Before this, the ship was used by the Egyptian postal service.

I also learned that Commander Gorringe's first name is Henry. The men say he was born in Barbados, which is an island just north of South America. He went to sea when he was 14 years old. He was caught in a storm & shipwrecked in India. Then he was rescued & got on a ship to Cuba where a kindly missionary arranged for him to come to America. After that, he fought in the American Civil War & became a Navy engineer. His life sounds a little like mine.

The men say that if Commander Gorringe successfully brings the obelisk to New York & stands it up there, he will be paid seventy-five thousand dollars! I cannot even imagine what it would be like to have that much money. But the money will be coming from someone who has even more of it—the richest man in America—William Henry Vanderbilt. His family made their fortune building railroads.

Seventy-five thousand dollars is a lot of money. But then, this is a big job. If Commander Gorringe fails, he gets nothing.

JULY 11, 1880

Many of the men in our crew, I have discovered, are drunkards. One of them fell overboard the other day, & we had to rescue him. Maybe that's why Commander Gorringe seems to like me so much. He has taken me under his wing. Yesterday, he pulled me aside & when he shook my hand, he slipped an American five dollar bill into it. He said he wanted to show his appreciation for plugging the leak in the boiler & replacing the broken crankshaft. He said I was indispensible, whatever that means. Commander Gorringe is a good man.

Forget about that hot dog I wanted to eat. The first thing I am going to do when we get to New York City is buy myself a big stake dinner with this five dollar bill. I will use whatever is left of the money to get some new clothes so I will look presentable when I apply for work in America.

JULY 12, 1880

Smooth sailing. We should be in New York in a few days. Everyone is excited that our voyage is nearly over. But I am concerned about the weather a head. The sky is darkening. It looks like we are in for a storm.

JULY 13, 1880

The wind kicked up, & it is getting stronger & stronger as the day goes on. I am afraid my diary will blow out of my hands or become soaked with water. We are tieing everything down so it will not blow away. Some of the men are seasick. Not me. I am used to being in rough waters.

The waves are getting bigger & the ship is bouncing up & down like an elevator. I have not been inside an elevator yet, but I know they go up

& down. I bet they have them in New York City. Maybe I will get to ride one when we get there.

I mean IF we get there.

JULY 14, 1880

It is getting worse. There are huge waterspouts forming not far from The Dessoug. They must be at least 50 feet high. If one of these waterspouts hits the ship, the weight of the water could smash the deck & it will be all over. They move so fast. It will not be possible to steer the ship around them. We have to hope for luck. Two giant waves have already broken on the deck. Everyone is slipping & hanging on to whatever they can grab.

The wind whips at my face so hard I can feel my cheeks being pulled. & now the rain is coming. The drops come down so hard they sting my face. Commander Gorringe has given the order to cover the hatches & skylights & get down below.

Now we are all huddling in the cargo hold with the obelisk. There is nothing we can do but wait it out. Men are saying prayers & writing letters to their loved ones. But if The Dessoug capsizes or breaks apart, none of those letters will be found. We will all be lost at sea. My diary will be gone.

Nobody will remember me, or any of us. The obelisk will be on the bottom of the Atlantic forever. Everything Commander Gorringe has worked so hard to achieve will be for nothing.

& then, for a moment, there was calm.

"Is it over?" somebody asked.

Commander Gorringe gave us permission to open the hatch & take a look outside. One by one we climbed the ladder up to the deck. It looked all clear. But then we turned around to see a waterspout behind The Dessoug. It was a giant funnel of swirling, furious water not more than 50 feet away. What holds it together? The waterspout looked like it was going to hit us dead on.

"Grab onto something!" shouted Commander Gorringe.

Then, at the last instant, the waterspout veered off in a different direction.

The storm is over. The sky calmed down. Nobody was hurt. Nobody fell overboard. But it was terrifying. We all pitched in to repair the damage. Commander Gorringe said we "dodged a bullet." I have never heard anyone say that before. We didn't dodge a real bullet, but it felt that way. I am thankful to be alive.

JULY 20, 1880

Finally! After 39 days at sea, early this morning we reached New York City! It is a busy, bustling port, much bigger than Alexandria. It is bigger than any city I have ever seen. It may even be bigger than London.

As we steamed into the harbor, passengers on ferryboats waved their hats & handkerchiefs at us. The newspapers must have told them we were coming.

The first thing we saw was a big, beautiful bridge that is not finished being built. They say it will be called the Brooklyn Bridge. They started building it 12 years ago, & it won't be done until 1883. That is a long time to build a bridge! Commander Gorringe says it will be the longest bridge in the world. He knows all about it because the company that made the steel cables for the bridge also made the cables for the machine he will use to stand the obelisk up in Central Park.

I thought we were going to go straight to that park, but apparently the water is too shallow to unload the obelisk near there. So instead, we docked at an island called Staten. I guess we are going to take the obelisk off The Dessoug here &

move it to another boat that can travel in shallower water.

There was a welcoming committee to greet us on the Staten island. Well, they were there to greet Commander Gorringe, anyway. Visitors were allowed on the Dessoug, & it looked like thousands of people came on to get a peek at the obelisk.

Everybody wanted to see the obelisk.

Before we got off the ship, Commander Gorringe pulled me aside again. I thought he was going to give me more money, or maybe take back the 5 dollars he gave me last week. But it was neither of those things. He offered me a job!

Commander Gorringe told me that some of the men he had hired in Egypt had already deserted. He also said bringing the obelisk across the ocean was only the beginning of his work. Now he would need a strong team of men to help him tow the obelisk up the river, bring it ashore, drag it halfway across the island of Manhattan, & stand it up in Central Park. & he needs a smart young man like me to help. That is what he called me—a smart young man.

He said it might take the rest of the year to finish. The pay would be 9 dollars a week plus room & board. That is pretty good wages.

I thought about it. The rest of the year is five months. That's a long time. Commander Gorringe is a good man & I would learn a lot working for him. But I decided to say no.

"Thank you," I told him. "But if America is the land of opportunity, I am going to take my chances on it right now."

"Good luck to you, Thomas," he said as he shook my hand. "I know you won't need it."

"Good luck with the obelisk," I told him.

I walked down the gangplank & headed... who knows where? I don't know where my future will take me, but I am glad I got the chance to come to America & I am glad I was able to write about it & keep it in my memory forever. I am anxious to eat a stake dinner, & lots of hot dogs.

You know, I think my speling is a lot better now than it was when I started this diary.

MEANWHILE, IN THE PRESENT DAY...

It was getting dark out. I looked at my mother and asked her, "Is all of this stuff true? Or did you just make it up? How do you know any of this stuff?"

"I have my secrets," she replied.

My mother looked at her watch and shook her head. I knew she was going to say we had to leave if we wanted to catch the train back to New Jersey.

"You can't stop *now*!" I told her. "What happened after Cleopatra's Needle got to Staten Island? How did Gorringe get it here, in the middle of Central Park?"

"Do you really want to know?" Mom asked me.

"Yes!" I said. "Don't leave me hanging!"

PART 5

I AM AN INVENTOR.
THIS IS MY STORY.

(1879–1881)

Diary of Rebecca Watson, a girl in New York City who witnessed Cleopatra's Needle being brought to Central Park

TUESDAY, JUNE 17, 1879

Dear Diary,

I have obelisk fever! Everybody does! I've never been so excited in my life!

Why am I excited, Diary? Well, some big news was announced today in The New York World newspaper. An ancient Egyptian obelisk called "Cleopatra's Needle" is coming to New York City! Isn't that wonderful?

It's only fair, I think. London has an Egyptian obelisk. Paris has an Egyptian obelisk. We're a big city too. New York should have an obelisk of our own.

I love everything to do with Egypt—the pyramids, the Sphinx, mummies. Maybe I'll become an archeologist someday. Then I'll go to Egypt and find the tomb of King Tut. It's got to be there, hidden somewhere under the sand. It's only a matter of time until somebody finds it.

But until then, I'll get to see Cleopatra's Needle because it's coming here. I don't know where they're going to put it, and I don't know when it will arrive. But I'll make sure to be there when it does.

This is probably the biggest thing to happen

around here since the Civil War ended and President Lincoln was tragically killed. That was almost fifteen years ago. I wasn't even born yet, so of course I don't remember. That's why this is <u>doubly</u> exciting! Because this will be a happy occasion rather than such a sad one, the way it was when the President died.

I'm going to pester my parents so they'll take me to see Cleopatra's Needle when it arrives. I know what I can do! I'll write a report for school about Cleopatra's Needle. Yes! Then Mom and Dad will <u>have</u> to let me go see it. They love anything that's educational.

WEDNESDAY, JUNE 18, 1879

I decided that I'm going to devote this diary to Cleopatra's Needle coming to New York. I promise to write about it, Dear Diary, <u>every day</u>.

THURSDAY, JANUARY 1, 1880

Dear Diary,

I am <u>sooooo</u> sorry I haven't written a word here in over five months. There hasn't been anything in the news about Cleopatra's Needle, so I haven't had anything to write. But today is the start of a

<u>new</u> year, and a new decade. I hope the obelisk will be here before the end of the year.

TUESDAY, JANUARY 27, 1880
Dear Diary,

Big news! I read in the newspaper that Mr. Thomas Edison of New Jersey has invented a lamp that runs on electricity instead of oil. Isn't that exciting? Soon we'll have electric lights in our house, in school, and even on the <u>street</u>!

Mr. Edison is my favorite inventor. When I grow up I want to be just like <u>him</u>. People say girls can't be inventors. I say why not? I don't care what anyone says. I'm going to <u>do</u> it. People also say you can achieve anything if you put your mind to it.

A few years ago, Mr. Edison invented an amazing machine called a phonograph. It's a about the size of a bread box, and it can record sounds and play them back just like they sounded in the first place. Isn't that <u>incredible</u>?

Now Mr. Edison says that in a few years he'll be able to make moving pictures. Can you imagine? Photographs that <u>move</u>? It seems impossible, but until Mr. Edison came along, nobody thought we could record sound or use electricity to make light. So I think he will do it.

Of course, people say lots of silly things about what we'll have in the future. I've read that soon we won't even use horses anymore to get around. We'll have carriages with engines in them powered by gasoline. I'll believe it when I see it. Personally, I'd be sad if we didn't have horses anymore. What will happen to our horses?

I've even heard people say that someday we'll have machines that can <u>fly</u>. I'm not joking, Diary! They say we'll be able to sit inside a machine that can lift up into the air under its own power and fly around from place to place! That sounds pretty dangerous to me. But this is why I want to become an inventor when I grow up. Inventors create things that change the way we live.

TUESDAY, MARCH 30, 1880
Dear Diary,

I invented my first invention today! My aunts and uncles and cousins were over for dinner and the table was crowded with food. It was hard to pass things back and forth across the big table. I suggested that if we put the food on a big wheel that could spin around, everybody could just take what they wanted without having to reach across the table.

After dinner I found two big boards in the basement. I used my father's little coping saw to cut them into circles. That was really hard, because wood wants to be cut in a straight line. But I did it. Then I drilled a hole in the middle of the two big circles and put a little post in there, like the axle of a wheel. Finally, I took a bunch of marbles and put them between the two circles so the top circle could spin around. We will try it out tomorrow when Annie's family is coming over for dinner.

WEDNESDAY, MARCH 31, 1880

We tried out my new invention at dinner tonight. It worked like a charm! Annie's mother liked it so much that she asked me to make one for their family too. Now I'm an inventor just like Mr. Edison!

THURSDAY, JUNE 14, 1880

Dear Diary,

School is out. Hooray! I like school, but I also like summer vacation. I'm going to spend a lot of time with my best friend, Annie Higgins.

Finally, there was a mention of Cleopatra's Needle in the newspaper today. The ship carrying it here has left Egypt. I can only imagine how difficult it will be to take a two-hundred-ton piece of stone and move it across the Atlantic Ocean.

All kinds of rumors are flying around. Some people say Cleopatra's Needle is going to be placed near Columbus Circle, at 59th Street. Annie says they're going to put it on 96th Street. Personally, I hope it'll be closer to 34th Street, where we live. Then I'll be able to see it any time I want.

SUNDAY, JUNE 20, 1880

Dear Diary,

I just got the news. They're going to place Cleopatra's Needle in Central Park behind the new Metropolitan Museum of Art! Right now, there's nothing but farms and vacant lots out there. It's in the middle of nowhere.

But that's okay. I figured it out. I live at 34th Street, and the Needle will be at 80th Street. 80 minus 34 is 46. So the Needle will be 46 blocks away from my house. There are twenty blocks in a mile. So Cleopatra's Needle will be a little more than two miles away from my house. That's not so far. If only Mom and Dad would buy me a bicycle, I could ride up there in no time.

I was afraid Cleopatra's Needle would be put inside the museum or some other building, and it would cost money to see it. That would be a shame. But when it's in Central Park, anyone will be able to go see it at any time, for free.

They're going to put Cleopatra's Needle in a part of Central Park called Graywacke Knoll, which is close to the east side of the park. It's quiet up there. Families will be able to take their horse and buggy over there and have a nice picnic at Cleopatra's Needle.

FRIDAY, JUNE 25, 1880

Dear Diary,

I read in the newspaper that the ship carrying Cleopatra's Needle is called The Dessoug. That's a funny name for a ship. It should be here in less than a month. I can't wait!

THURSDAY, JULY 1, 1880

Dear Diary,

Guess what? I just found out that *another* big monument is coming to New York City! The

French-American Union just announced that they've raised enough money to finish building Liberty, that statue of the lady holding a torch up in the air. They're building the statue right now, and it may take five years for her to arrive. But then she's going to stand in New York Harbor to welcome people from all over the world.

Soon she will be finished!

MONDAY, JULY 19, 1880

Dear Diary,

Today is the day! Cleopatra's Needle is due to arrive in New York. The newspaper said the ship is going to dock in Staten Island first. I want to go there to see it, but Mom and Dad said no. <u>Boo</u>! They never let me go anywhere.

TUESDAY, JULY 20, 1880

Dear Diary,

It's in all the newspapers—The Dessoug is docked at 23rd Street. Cleopatra's Needle is less than ten blocks from us! Annie and I rushed over there. As it turned out, there was nothing to see. Cleopatra's Needle is still inside The Dessoug. But lots of people went there anyway. Somebody said there were almost two thousand people. All the ferryboat passengers were waving their hats and hankies.

WEDNESDAY, JULY 21, 1880

Dear Diary,

The Dessoug docked at 51st Street today. We thought they were going to unload Cleopatra's Needle there, but no. A crane on the dock lifted some big blocks of stone off the ship and swung them on to the shore. The blocks turned out to be the pedestal, the steps, and the foundation that are going to sit under Cleopatra's Needle. A police officer told me they need to put those things in place first. That makes sense.

They put the pedestal on this big cart at 51st Street.

The pedestal was lowered onto a big truck wagon. I counted sixteen pairs of horses in front of the wagon—that's thirty-two horses! I guess they need a lot of horse power to move the stone across Manhattan to Central Park. The pedestal looks soooooo heavy.

After they loaded up the wagon, it moved very slowly across 51st Street. Annie and I watched for a while. The workers had to stop two or three times because the wheels sank into the pavement. Or is it "sunk"? Anyway, the horses looked like they were working really hard to pull the wheels out of the grooves in the street. That's how heavy the wagon is—and that's only the pedestal!

I haven't seen Cleopatra's Needle itself yet, but I did see the man who is in charge of bringing it here from Egypt. His name is Lieutenant Commander Henry Gorringe, and all the newspapers are talking about him. Mr. Gorringe must be a very smart man. I saw him directing the workers at the truck wagon. He seems very calm and in charge.

And do you know what Mr. Gorringe's middle name is, Diary? Honychurch! Isn't that adorable?

Annie said we should go over to Mr. Gorringe and ask for his autograph. But I'm afraid. He seems so busy all the time. I would hate to bother him while he's working so hard.

FRIDAY, JULY 23, 1880

Dear Diary,

Cleopatra's Needle is becoming a Broadway star! They're selling all kinds of silly things with pictures of obelisks on them. This morning I passed by a candy stand where a man was selling "Cleopatra dates." They were in obelisk-shaped boxes. And there's a new drink at restaurants called "the Obbylish." I want to try one, but Mom said it's a drink for grownups.

At our local sewing shop, you can buy Cleopatra's Needle thread and other goodies. I saw a lady wearing a necklace that had a silver pencil shaped like Cleopatra's Needle. I <u>want</u> one!

Annie and I went over to Greywacke Knoll today, where the Needle is going to stand forever. It's one of the highest points in Central Park. We watched the workers cutting down some trees in the area, which was sad. Afterward, we went to the Metropolitan Museum of Art and looked at the Egyptian artifacts. It's hard to believe some of them are over three thousand years old.

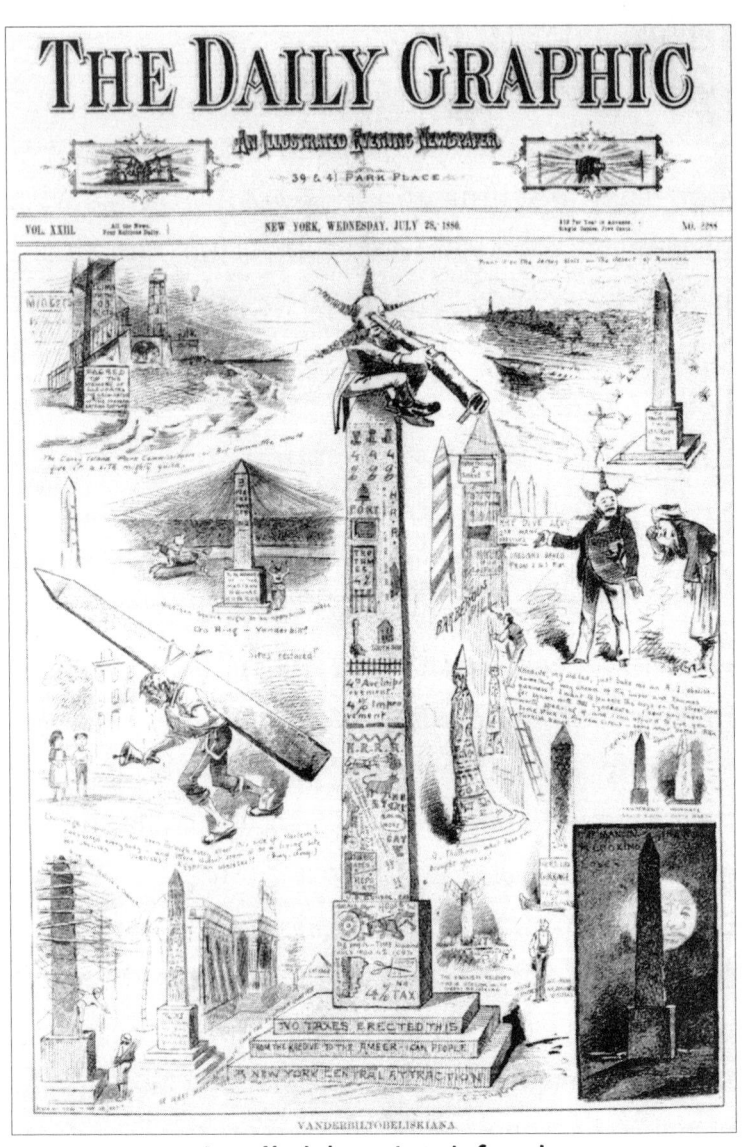

New York has obelisk fever!

THURSDAY, AUGUST 5, 1880

Dear Diary,

Everybody's following the progress of Cleopatra's Needle in the newspaper. Annie and I watched the workmen prepare the ground at Greywacke Knoll. They shoveled off the topsoil, and then they leveled the surface and filled the cracks in with concrete. They need to make it perfect and flat so Cleopatra's Needle can stand up straight. After three thousand years, it would be <u>horrible</u> if it toppled over and broke in half!

The workers took a long time getting the ground ready. It was boring so we left.

THURSDAY, SEPTEMBER 16, 1880

Dear Diary,

Now I know why they took Cleopatra's Needle to Staten Island instead of bringing it straight to Manhattan. The newspapers say the man who owns the dock here wanted too much money and Mr. Gorringe refused to pay it. Good for him!

But today was a big day. My parents took me and Annie all the way to Staten Island to watch them unload Cleopatra's Needle from The Dessoug. We took a ferryboat, which was fun.

The Dessoug is a big ship. It has to be, with that giant obelisk inside. When we got there, everybody (including me) was wondering how they were going to get Cleopatra's Needle out of the ship. I couldn't imagine. How would they lift the boat up high enough?

Mr. Gorringe must be a very smart man. Do you know what he did to lift the boat up, Diary?

Nothing! He just waited until the high tide came in at four o'clock in the afternoon. Then the water lifted the boat up all by itself. Smart!

"Hurry!" I heard Mr. Gorringe shouting to the workmen.

I guess they had to move fast before the tide went out again. A bunch of workers rushed over to The Dessoug with tools, and they started unscrewing plates on the side of the hull. It was very interesting to watch! I didn't know it was possible to open up a boat like that.

We pushed closer to see it with our own eyes. Lots of people were there. We all wanted to catch the first glimpse of Cleopatra's Needle as it poked its pointy top out of The Dessoug.

I counted. They took off thirty plates, opening

up a big hole in the side of the boat. It was dark in there, so we couldn't see anything yet.

Before they could slide Cleopatra's Needle out of the ship, the workmen laid down metal tracks, sort of like railroad tracks. The tracks went all the way from the ship to the shore. They were closer together than regular railroad tracks. And do you know what they put on the tracks, Diary? Cannonballs! Isn't that <u>smart</u>? I guess it will be easier to roll Cleopatra's Needle out of the ship than it would be to drag it. The workmen built a little boardwalk next to The Dessoug.

It was time for the big moment. With all those people watching, it was hard to find a place to stand. Ropes were attached inside the ship and a bunch of strong men pulled on them. Suddenly this big pointy thing poked out of the ship. Everybody was cheering, even though we couldn't see the actual Cleopatra's Needle when it came through the hole because it is covered in wood. I guess that's to protect it, sort of like the way a pillowcase protects a pillow.

It was exciting to watch them roll the wooden

casing out of the ship. But we were still disappointed that we couldn't see the Needle itself. I cut this picture out of the newspaper to show the big moment.

Finally, they took Cleopatra's Needle off the ship.

After it was all the way out, the workmen rushed to rivet the plates back into place and close up the hole in The Dessoug. They wouldn't be able to sail that ship anywhere with a big hole in one side, of course.

We caught the ferry back to Manhattan. Annie and I were sad because summer vacation is over now. School starts tomorrow. I won't be able see Mr. Gorringe and his men bring Cleopatra's Needle to Central Park. Maybe Annie and I can go after school and on weekends.

FRIDAY, SEPTEMBER 17, 1880
Dear Diary,

I begged Mom and Dad to go to Staten Island again, but they said I have to go to school. They are <u>so</u> mean! I'll have to wait until Cleopatra's Needle gets to Manhattan. It should be here in about a week.

The New York Times says they're going to use a <u>different</u> boat to bring Cleopatra's Needle twelve miles up the Hudson River from Staten Island to 96th Street. It's called a pontoon boat. That's a boat with a flat bottom and big floats on each side. It doesn't have a motor. They're going to tow it behind a steamboat.

I don't quite understand why they have to switch boats, but there must be a reason. Maybe the water is too shallow at 96th Street for The Dessoug to dock there.

SATURDAY, SEPTEMBER 25, 1880

Dear Diary,

We are so lucky! Today is the day Cleopatra's Needle came to Manhattan, and it's Saturday so Annie and I were allowed to go to the Hudson River at 96th Street today to see it come ashore. We waited for *hours* with a bunch of other people. And then finally somebody shouted and we all looked to see the steamboat towing the pontoon boat up the river. Everybody was cheering and the other boats blasted their steam whistles as it approached 96th Street. Mr. Gorringe and his workmen had built a landing stage at the edge of the water.

While we waited, I told Annie that I'm going to become an inventor when I grow up. And do you know what she told me? She said that she's going to grow up and marry Mr. Gorringe! Isn't that the silliest thing you've ever heard?

It's true that Mr. Gorringe is handsome and has nice blue eyes. But he's at least twenty years older than we are! Annie said she calculated that when she's 35, Mr. Gorringe will be 55. And when she's 55, he'll be 75, and <u>that's</u> not so big a difference. Annie really likes Mr. Gorringe—and arithmetic.

After they positioned the pontoon boat at the edge of the water, the workmen attached the iron tracks with the cannonballs in them. This time they used a big engine with a winch and thick chains around a giant drum to drag Cleopatra's Needle off the boat. At <u>last</u>, it was on the island of Manhattan, on dry land! We were beside ourselves with joy.

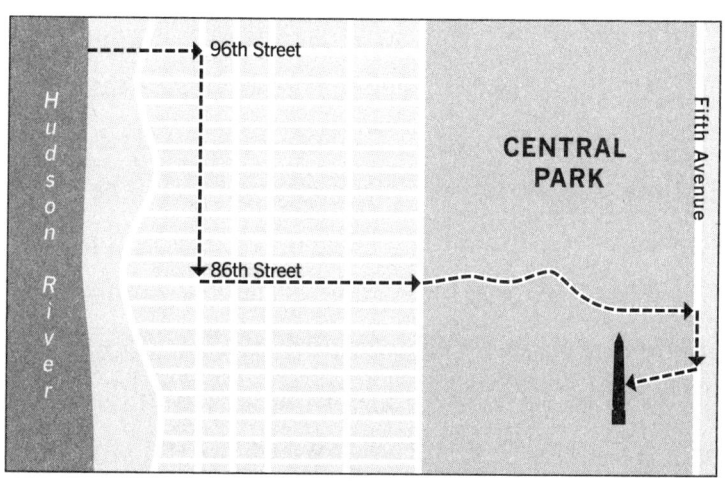

The route across Manhattan.

SUNDAY, SEPTEMBER 26, 1880

Dear Diary,

After church, Annie and I went to see how far Cleopatra's Needle had been moved since yesterday. Hardly at all! It was still sitting at 96th Street near the river. If you ask me, they should stand it up right there. That would be so <u>simple</u>. But they've decided to move it across Manhattan to Central Park. That's not going to be easy. But I believe that if anybody can do it, it will be Mr. Gorringe.

He has two teams of men working for him. We watched as one team put track on the ground in front of Cleopatra's Needle, and the other team picked up the track from behind it as it inched forward. It's very slow, but at least Cleopatra's Needle is moving now.

It takes so much time because 96th Street slopes up from the Hudson river so they have to drag Cleopatra's Needle <u>up</u>hill. They put big iron wedges behind it so it won't roll backward into the river. Can you imagine what a disaster <u>that</u> would be?

I feel sorry for the men who are doing the work. I hope they are getting paid fairly. Somebody said the work pays nine dollars a week, which is not so bad. It's more than most grownups earn, anyway.

Then I thought of <u>another</u> problem. A train line

goes up and down Manhattan very close to the Hudson River! It runs every hour or so, even on Sundays. I was wondering what would happen if the train arrived while Cleopatra's Needle was crossing the little bridge they put over the tracks. That would be a disaster if a train collided with Cleopatra's Needle.

Annie told me she heard that Mr. William Vanderbilt, the millionaire who's paying Mr. Gorringe to bring Cleopatra's Needle here, owns the railroad. So he can stop a train whenever he wants to. One freight train did come along while they were pulling the obelisk over the tracks, but it was only delayed a half an hour or so.

The train stopping for Cleopatra's Needle at 96th Street.

SATURDAY, OCTOBER 9, 1880
Dear Diary,

Annie and I could have gone back to 96th Street today. But we decided to go see the parade on Fifth Avenue instead. The newspaper said nine thousand Freemasons were marching, and thirty thousand people lined the street to welcome Cleopatra's Needle to New York. There were bands playing, flags waving, and lots of horses and carriages.

The parade ended at Greywacke Knoll, where there was a big ceremony. There were men in top hats and white gloves standing on a platform built just for them.

The funny thing is, Cleopatra's Needle isn't even at Central Park yet. Mr. Gorringe and his men are still dragging it across 96th Street. The parade was just to celebrate the cornerstone being put in the foundation that will go <u>under</u> the obelisk.

This is the interesting part, Diary. Along with the cornerstone, the workmen buried a time capsule in the steps of the foundation. It's inside a lead box that was sealed with concrete to keep air out. I guess the time capsule will show people hundreds of years from now what life was like in

1880. Do you want to know what they put inside the time capsule? I made a list. . . .

—*Some 1880 coins*
—*Webster's dictionary*
—*The complete works of William Shakespeare*
—*The Bible, in various languages*
—*A copy of the Declaration of Independence*
—*A New York City directory and map*
—*The 1870 census*
—*Some presidential medals*

And probably some other stuff too. I heard they wanted to put Mr. Bell's marvelous new telephone inside the time capsule, but they couldn't get one. Too bad. Annie said that maybe they could put a telephone in later, but I don't know how they'll be able to open up the time capsule after Cleopatra's Needle is standing on top of it! The time capsule and all the things inside it may be under there <u>forever</u>.

Oh, I almost forgot, Diary. Do you want to know a secret? Before they sealed up the foundation, Mr. William Hurlbert, the editor of The World, walked over and put one more thing inside. It was a small box. A <u>secret</u> box. <u>Nobody</u> knows what's inside it. Well, Mr. Hurlbert knows, I suppose. But he's not saying what it is.

I love a mystery! Everybody is trying to guess what's in the box.

SUNDAY, OCTOBER 10, 1880

Dear Diary,

Believe it or not, they're still dragging Cleopatra's Needle across 96th Street. It takes so long! So Annie and I went to Greywacke Knoll to see what was happening. We got there just in time to see the men using a big crane to lift up the fifty-ton pedestal, swing it over the foundation, and lower it in place.

One of the workmen told me they were instructed to place the foundation in exactly in the same direction as it had been when it was in Egypt. I don't see why that matters, but I guess they had their reasons.

Before we left, I asked a worker when he expected Cleopatra's Needle would be standing up at Greywacke Knoll, and he said it could be months.

<u>Months</u>?!

WEDNESDAY, OCTOBER 27, 1880

Dear Diary,

    I have a confession to make. Annie and I told our parents we were going to school today, but we played hooky instead. I know it's wrong and I feel bad about lying. But I read in the newspaper that Mr. Gorringe is having serious problems moving Cleopatra's Needle, so I had to go uptown to see what was going on.

    When I got to 96th Street, I felt sad for Mr. Gorringe and his men. They are working so hard. It took a month just to move a few blocks. The rails they have been using keep breaking under the weight of Cleopatra's Needle. It must be <u>soooo</u> heavy.

    They reached West Boulevard today and they're trying to make a right turn there. I can't imagine how they're going to do it. It's hard enough for them to move in a straight line. But I hope Mr. Gorringe will figure it out.

THURSDAY, OCTOBER 28, 1880

    My parents found out that I played hooky yesterday. They were really mad. Now I can't go out for the rest of the week. I am heartbroken.

SUNDAY, OCTOBER 31, 1880

Dear Diary,

Today is Halloween, so my parents said my punishment is over and I can go out again. Naturally, I went to see Cleopatra's Needle.

Finally, they were able to turn the corner onto West Boulevard. It took six days (and nights)! Mr. Gorringe looked tired, worried, and a little angry. The weather is starting to get cold, and I know he wanted to have Cleopatra's Needle in place by the end of the year. That's not going to happen if it takes six days just to turn a corner.

But here's the best part, Diary. We were invited over to Annie's house for Halloween dinner. And you'll never believe who was there.

Mr. Henry Honychurch Gorringe!!!

I did not make that up! He is a friend of a friend of Annie's father so they invited him over. I was nervous sitting across the table from Mr. Gorringe, and I didn't say anything for the longest time. The grownups were talking about Cleopatra's Needle and Mr. Gorringe said how frustrating it was to spend six days turning the corner on to West Boulevard.

That's when Annie's mom started bringing out

the plates of food and putting them on the table. After she put each plate down, she spun the invention I made for her, to make room for the next plate.

I saw that Mr. Gorringe was watching intently as Annie's mom put the food on the table.

"Where did you get that thing?" he finally asked.

"It was Rebecca's idea," said Annie's mom as she pointed at me. "She invented it."

Mr. Gorringe turned to look at me.

"Passing plates back and forth across the table is a pain in the neck," I told him. "So I figured that putting them on a big wheel would make things easier."

"And what did you put between the two wheels to enable the top one to turn around?" he asked.

"Marbles," I replied.

Mr. Gorringe looked at my invention for a long time.

"What do you call this?" he asked me.

"Uh," I said, "it's a table that turns. So I guess I call it a turntable."

"That's it!" he exclaimed.

"What's it?" I asked.

"You have given me a very good idea, young lady," he said. And then he quickly gathered up his coat and hat and left.

That was strange. After dinner, we celebrated Halloween by telling ghost stories around the fireplace. Then we bobbed for apples and had cider and doughnuts. Yummy!

MONDAY, NOVEMBER 1, 1880

Today was absolutely the best day of my life, Diary. After school, Annie and I went uptown to see where Cleopatra's Needle was. And do you know what we saw when we got to 86th Street? A giant turntable that looked a lot like my invention was sitting in the middle of the street! It had a circular metal track underneath it with cannonballs (not marbles) in the track. The workers were dragging Cleopatra's Needle onto it.

As soon as he saw me, Mr. Gorringe ran over and thanked me for giving him the idea of the turntable.

"You <u>must</u> allow me to compensate you for your idea," he said, pulling his wallet out of his pocket.

"Pay me?" I never expected to get any money

for my invention. I thanked him and said there was no need to pay me. I just wanted to do what I could to help bring Cleopatra's Needle to New York City. Annie looked so jealous when Mr. Gorringe gave me a big hug.

"This is the moment of truth," he whispered in my ear.

Once Cleopatra's Needle was in the middle of the turntable, Mr. Gorringe gave the workers the order to turn it. Ten of them took positions around the turntable and started to push it. At first it didn't move. I was afraid it wasn't going to work. Maybe Cleopatra's Needle was just too heavy. But then, suddenly, there was a creaking noise and the wheel began to slowly turn. It wasn't long before it had made a quarter turn and Cleopatra's Needle was facing east along 86th Street.

"It works!" somebody shouted.

Everybody was saying how it had taken six days to turn the first corner, but only a few minutes to turn this one.

"And this is the young lady who invented the device," Mr. Gorringe announced as he pointed to me. Everybody clapped and I took a bow.

I'm an inventor!

TUESDAY, NOVEMBER 2, 1880

Dear Diary,

Today was Election Day and everyone was excited. My father voted for Mr. Winfield Hancock. My mother said that if women were allowed to vote, she would vote for Mr. James Garfield. If I could vote, I would vote for Mr. Garfield too. His wife is named Lucretia, and that is my cousin's name.

We don't know who won yet, but the winner will be the 20th president of the United States. I wonder if Mr. Gorringe voted today. Every time we come to watch, he's always working. I can't imagine him taking a rest to go vote.

THURSDAY, NOVEMBER 11, 1880

They moved the Cleopatra's Needle six hundred feet today—the best day so far. Mr. Gorringe and the workers seemed happy. Maybe they will be able to finish the job before the year ends.

While the men were working, Annie and I walked across Central Park to Greywacke Knoll. The workers there are assembling two tall wooden structures on either side of the pedestal. Everybody says that when Cleopatra's Needle arrives in the park, they're going to put an iron belt around it and the wooden structure will turn the obelisk so it stands upright. It seems hard to believe that will be possible, but I have to believe Mr. Gorringe knows what he's doing.

SATURDAY, NOVEMBER 13, 1880
Dear Diary,

Cleopatra's Needle is slowly making its way across 86th Street. Soon it will reach Central Park. I'm so excited! I wish I had a camera so I could take a photograph of it and paste it here, Diary. But cameras are very expensive and the only people who own them are professional photographers.

SATURDAY, NOVEMBER 20, 1880
Dear Diary,

With each passing day there are more people gathering to watch Cleopatra's Needle as it moves across Manhattan. Not fair! Annie and I were here first.

A few of them are bad people too. I've heard that some souvenir hunters were caught hanging around near Cleopatra's Needle late at night with hammers and chisels. They planned to chip off pieces and sell them as souvenirs. Isn't that just <u>awful</u>? Why do people do things like that?

Luckily, Mr. Gorringe has guards surrounding Cleopatra's Needle day and night. He thinks of everything.

THURSDAY, NOVEMBER 25, 1880
Dear Diary,

Cleopatra's Needle has made it to Central Park, and just in time for Thanksgiving! Mr. Gorringe gave his workmen a day off to spend time with their families. But soon the obelisk will be on its pedestal, standing tall for all to see. I can't wait.

SUNDAY, DECEMBER 5, 1880
Dear Diary,

Getting across Central Park is taking longer than I expected. The city streets are smooth and flat. But the park is filled with hills, trees, and boulders that the workmen have to avoid.

Mr. Gorringe has one team of workers that starts at six o'clock in the morning, and another team replaces them at dinnertime. And Mr. Gorringe is supervising both teams all the time. I don't know when he sleeps or where he gets so much energy.

Also, it's getting really cold out now. It has snowed the last few days. The poor workmen look exhausted, and I've heard that some of them have come down with rheumatism. Some have just quit because the work is so hard. I haven't heard that any of them died, thank goodness. Annie told me she read that six men died when the British brought their obelisk to London a few years ago.

SUNDAY, DECEMBER 16, 1880
Dear Diary,

Cleopatra's Needle reached Fifth Avenue today. It took nineteen days to get across Central Park. They set up the big turntable (you're welcome!) on Fifth Avenue and turned the obelisk so it's facing downtown. Just a few more blocks and it will be at Greywacke Knoll. Almost there!

SATURDAY, DECEMBER 18, 1880
Dear Diary,

Cleopatra's Needle is at 82nd Street. I thought that they were just going to drag it the short distance from Fifth Avenue to Greywacke Knoll, but they didn't. Greywacke Knoll is higher than Fifth Avenue, and they have to raise the obelisk about fifty feet to get it into position. The hill is too steep to drag it up.

So do you know what they're doing? They're building a railroad trestle! It's made out of thick timber. It should be finished any day now.

The railroad trestle at the edge of Central Park.

WEDNESDAY, DECEMBER 22, 1880

Dear Diary,

I had school so I couldn't go to Graywacke Knoll today. But the newspaper said they finished building the railroad trestle and they're going to put Cleopatra's Needle in place the day after Christmas. That's also my birthday! I can't think of a nicer present for me, for Central Park, and for New York City.

SATURDAY, DECEMBER 25, 1880

Merry Christmas and Happy Birthday to me! I guess it's your birthday too, Diary. I wish I could give you a present. But you're just a book, so I don't know what I can possibly give you, other than more words.

Guess what my parents gave me—a bicycle! It's a beautiful blue Mergomobile that's made out of wood, with solid rubber tires. None of my friends at school own a bicycle yet. I'm the first.

I've never been on a bicycle, but people say they're quite easy to ride once you get the hang of it. You power the Mergomobile by pushing the foot levers on either side of the frame. It will take me a while to learn how to ride it, but after Cleopatra's Needle is in position and the weather is warmer, I'll be able to ride my bicycle up to Central Park to see it whenever I want to.

My very own Mergomobile!

TUESDAY, DECEMBER 28, 1880

Dear Diary,

Today was the big day! Today was the big day! Today was the big day!

Except that it wasn't. Excitement has been building since Christmas. Thousands of people gathered in the park to see Cleopatra's Needle get raised up. The men wore their stovepipe hats, and the ladies showed up with their finest bonnets. And then do you know what happened?

A blizzard hit. I don't think I've ever seen so much snow. There must have been three feet on the ground. They say this is one of the coldest winters anyone can remember.

I hope this doesn't mean we'll have to wait until spring to see Cleopatra's Needle standing up. We've waited so long already. Mr. Gorringe has suspended work for a few days, but who knows how long it will be?

SATURDAY, JANUARY 1, 1881

Dear Diary,

Happy New Year! I can't believe it's 1881. It seems like only a year ago that we were celebrating the beginning of 1880! Just joking, Diary.

Mr. Gorringe wasn't able to finish the job in time for New Year's, but what could he do? Weather is weather. The snow finally stopped coming down and it is starting to melt. Annie and I didn't go to Central Park today because we knew Mr. Gorringe was not going to make his men work on New Year's Day.

In the meantime, I just read in the paper that they're building a canal that's going to go through Panama. It will be fifty miles long. Can you believe it? Ships used to have to go all the way around South America to get from New York to San Francisco. When the canal is finished, that trip will be much faster.

This is why I'm going to become an inventor. Inventors invent things to make life easier for people.

WEDNESDAY, JANUARY 5, 1881

Dear Diary,

After school, Annie and I watched as Mr. Gorringe and his men moved Cleopatra's Needle into position. The middle of the obelisk is now positioned right over the pedestal.

Well, not the exact middle. It's what they call "the center of gravity." You see, an obelisk is thicker on the bottom than it is on the top. So if you tried to turn it from the exact middle point, one end would be heavier than the other and the whole thing would topple over. But if you turn it at the center of gravity, it's easy to turn because there's an equal amount of weight on each side. That's science.

I read in the newspaper that the center of gravity is twenty-six feet from the bottom of Cleopatra's Needle. I don't know how they calculate that, but I'm sure I'll learn when I take advanced math classes in school.

Now all they have to do is turn Cleopatra's Needle until it's vertical. It has been almost nineteen months since I heard the obelisk was coming to New York, and 102 days since it arrived in Manhattan. I counted. They say good things are worth waiting for, Diary.

Before we went home, we watched for a while as the workmen started to take apart the railroad trestle. Now that Cleopatra's Needle is in place, they won't need it anymore.

THURSDAY, JANUARY 20, 1881

Dear Diary,

The turning mechanism is finished. It's hard to believe that a bunch of pieces of wood and iron screwed together will be strong enough to hold up a 220-ton piece of stone and turn it from horizontal to vertical. I heard the turning mechanism weighs more than a ton, and it was made melted-down metal from cannons captured from the Confederacy during the Civil War. Everybody trusts that Mr. Gorringe knows what he's doing. He's going to turn Cleopatra's Needle and put it on its pedestal any day now. I am <u>so</u> excited!

FRIDAY, JANUARY 21, 1881
Dear Diary,
    The word is out. It's going to be <u>tomorrow</u>. They're going to turn it <u>tomorrow</u>! How am I going to sleep tonight?

SATURDAY, JANUARY 22, 1881
Dear Diary,
    Guess what? There was another big snowstorm last night. I don't know how many inches we got, but there were a lot of them. We didn't know if Mr. Gorringe and his men were going to go ahead, but Annie and I decided to go to Central Park just in case. After waiting as long as we have, it would be horrible to miss the big event.

We got here early to get a good view, and I'm glad we did. There are <u>thousands</u> of people here! And they're still streaming in. It will be hard to get a good view.

Kids are sledding on the hills in Central Park. I brought you, Diary, with me so I can write in you as it's happening. It wouldn't be fair to leave you home.

I still haven't seen Cleopatra's Needle itself. It's been covered with wooden boards the whole time. I certainly hope they'll take that wood off soon so we can see the obelisk. We've been waiting so patiently.

Even with all the snow on the ground, it looks like they're going to go ahead. Hooray! The park is beautiful covered in snow. It's very cold out. I can see my breath. Fortunately, I bundled up good. I can see icicles hanging off the wooden casing of Cleopatra's Needle. Some people have built bonfires to keep warm. There are lots of carriages and horses here. I feel sorry for those horses, having to stand in the cold. They don't know what's going on.

I just spotted Mr. Gorringe. He looks very handsome in his black overcoat and top hat. Wait! He's coming over here!

"It would be my honor, Rebecca, to have you and your family view the proceedings from the grandstand," he just told me. "After all, we wouldn't be here today if not for you."

He actually said those words to me! I'm so happy!

Mr. Gorringe led us to a grandstand on the north side of Cleopatra's Needle. We have the best seat in the house! There are a bunch of important looking dignitaries dressed up in fine clothes. Oooh, the Marine Band just marched over from Fifth Avenue. They're playing The Obelisk Waltz.

Mr. Gorringe is shaking hands with a bunch of big shots, and now he's going down to talk to the workmen. At least ten of them are gathered around him. A hush has fallen over the crowd.

I count seven small hydraulic jacks attached to the bottom of Cleopatra's Needle. Mr. Gorringe gave the word, and they pushed Cleopatra's Needle up a few feet off the trestle! It looks like it's suspended in the air.

Now they're clamping Cleopatra's Needle to the turning mechanism. Mr. Gorringe is walking

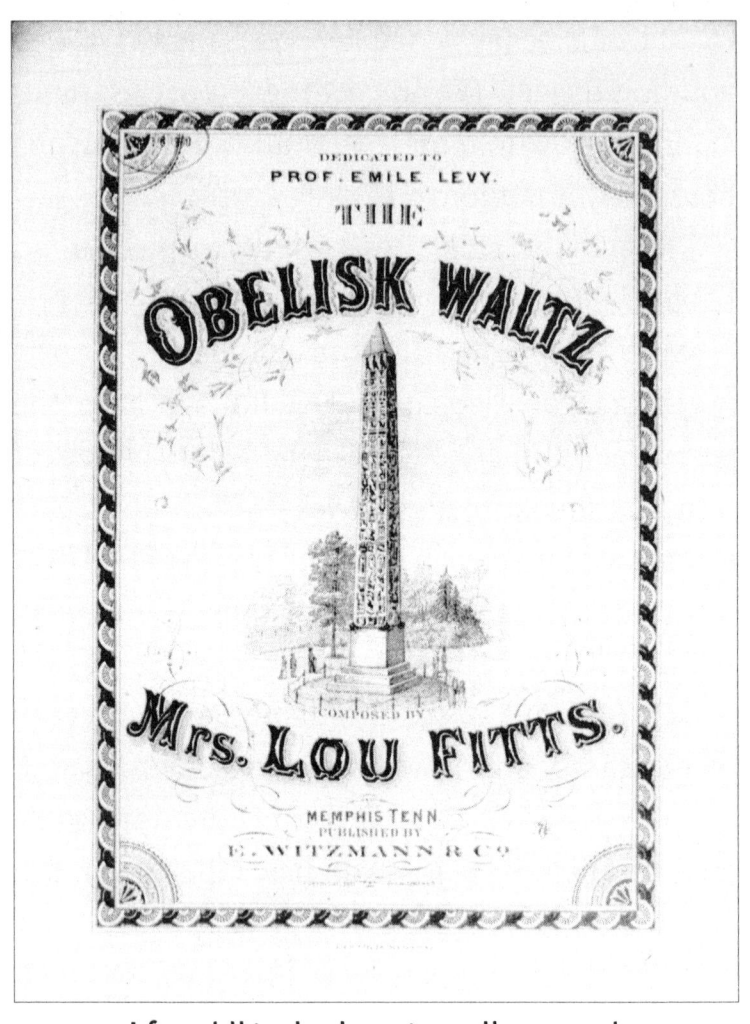

I found this sheet music on the ground.

around to look at it from all sides and make sure it's clamped on tightly.

It's almost noon. That's when the newspapers said Cleopatra's Needle would be turned vertical.

Two groups of workmen are grabbing the cables on either side of Cleopatra's Needle. Five in the front and five in the back.

Everybody's looking at Mr. Gorringe. Diary, I am going to have to stop writing. I don't want to miss anything!

The big moment.

Mr. Gorringe just put his hand up in the air.

He's holding a handkerchief.

The workmen are pulling on the cables.

It's totally silent except for the workmen grunting! I'm holding my breath.

The pointy end of the Needle is starting to lift up! The bottom end is swinging down!

It's turning! It's <u>turning</u>! I can't believe five men pulling on ropes can turn something that weighs over two hundred tons!

It's at a 45-degree angle! It's unbelievable!

Cleopatra's Needle is standing up, straight and tall!

We all broke out in cheers. Everybody is shaking hands and hugging. The Marine band is playing. Annie said that Cleopatra's Needle is so high, it looks like it's scraping against the sky. I said it must be a skyscraper.

I can't believe it took over a year to get Cleopatra's Needle from Egypt to America. And then it took just five minutes to turn it vertical. It's <u>amazing</u>!

Some men just ran over and placed big bronze sculptures of crabs at the four corners of the pedestal. I guess that will give it extra support.

Oh, they're peeling off the wooden casing now! It's about time. As they take off each board and toss it to the ground, I can see more and more of Cleopatra's Needle. Oh, it is a beautiful thing.

There are interesting symbols called hieroglyphs that are carved into the sides of the obelisk. The newspapers have been talking about them for weeks. They say the symbols are secret messages from the ancient Egyptians. I don't know about that. But the hieroglyphs do make Cleopatra's Needle even more interesting to look at.

I can hardly believe I was lucky enough to witness this amazing event. Someday, when I grow up and have children of my own, I'm going to bring them here to see this and tell them how I watched Mr. Henry Honychurch Gorringe bring Cleopatra's Needle to Central Park. And maybe someday, they'll bring their children and grandchildren too.

Cleopatra's Needle in Central Park today.

MEANWHILE, IN THE PRESENT DAY...

"Well, that's the whole story," Mom said as she got up from the bench. "If we hurry, I think we can be home in time for dinner—"

"Wait a minute!" I shouted. "Did you just say 'they'll bring their children'? Does that mean that the girl who wrote the last diary was..."

"My great-grandmother," my mom said. "Your great-great grandmother."

My mind was blown.

"Why didn't you tell me from the start that your great-grandmother was here when they brought Cleopatra's Needle to America?"

"You didn't seem all that interested," Mom replied. "And I didn't want to bore you. You said you wanted to go home and watch a ball game on TV."

"But now I want to know what happened next!" I whined. "What was in the secret box that guy stashed under Cleopatra's Needle? Is it still there? What happened to the *Dessoug*? What happened after the obelisk got here?"

"You ask too many questions," Mom said as we left Central Park. "Maybe we'll come back another time and I'll tell you about all those things."

Well, I didn't want to wait to get the rest of the story. I wanted to find out what happened right away. So I looked it up for myself. Isn't that why they invented the internet?

So here's what I found out:

- In 1881, the summer after Cleopatra's Needle was raised in Central Park, the mummy of Thutmosis III was found in a secret burial chamber in a cave high up on a cliff in Egypt. Mummies of forty other pharaohs and royals were found there too, and they were put into Egyptian museums. So the same year Cleopatra's Needle found a new home, so did the pharaoh who was responsible for making it.

  And in 1922, King Tut's tomb was finally found.

- After delivering Cleopatra's Needle to New York City, the *Dessoug* was used for shipping cotton and coal between New York and Savannah, Georgia. When I searched online, some sources said its propeller broke in the 1890s and the ship was turned into scrap metal. Other sources said it was lost at sea.

Nobody seems to know for sure what happened to it. It may be underwater somewhere in the Atlantic Ocean today.

- I'd like to tell you what was inside that mysterious box that William Hurlbert put inside the foundation of Cleopatra's Needle, but I can't. To this day, *nobody* knows what's inside it. The box is still sitting there, as it has been for over a hundred and forty years. So are all the other objects that were placed in the foundation. Maybe someday we'll have the technology to peek under there and see what's inside.

- By 1885, Cleopatra's Needle was already dirty from the pollution and cold weather in New York City. Today, the pink color is gone, the surface is rough, and some of the hieroglyphs are hard to see. Over the years, efforts have been made to clean and preserve the obelisk. It's been treated with wax, oils, detergent, and lasers. There's been talk of moving it indoors, building a glass dome over it, or even returning it to Egypt.

There have also been rumors about it. In 1932, people predicted that Cleopatra's

Needle was going to crumble just before a solar eclipse.

Despite it all, the obelisk is still there. It looks like it could fall over pretty easily, but it's been calculated that it would take a wind force of seventy-eight tons to knock it over. A typical hurricane is fifteen tons of wind force. So Cleopatra's Needle will probably be right where it is for a good long time.

FACTS AND FICTIONS

Everything in this book is true, except for the stuff I made up. It's only fair to tell you which is which. First, the fake stuff. The boys and girls who "wrote" these diaries are fictional characters. There are no such kids, and there are no such diaries. Sorry!

- So Zosar Zuberi did *not* help carve Cleopatra's Needle out of its granite bed. But hundreds and maybe thousands of laborers worked in the granite quarries of Aswan carving obelisks just as I described in Part 1. There's some debate about whether they were paid workers, criminals, prisoners of war, enslaved people, or a combination of all four. I consulted with Egyptologist Dr. Bob Brier, author of the excellent book *Cleopatra's Needles: The Lost Obelisks of Egypt*. He told me, "When the Egyptians went into battle and defeated a foreign country, they took prisoners back to Egypt to be servants in temples, etc. They are usually called 'prisoners,' but certainly could be viewed as 'enslaved.' If you get any grief for the use of 'slave,' feel free to invoke my name."

- So Lateef Jabari did *not* draw the hieroglyphs for Cleopatra's Needle. We don't know who did. We also don't know how accurate his description is of standing the obelisks up by building then removing big hills of sand. The ancient Egyptians didn't leave detailed records, so we'll never know for sure exactly how the obelisks were designed, carved, inscribed, or erected. But *somebody* did all these things with technology that seems so primitive to us today. The only theory I have read is that the Egyptians could have built giant sand hills, dragged the obelisks to the top, then dug pits in the sand hills to slide the obelisks into a standing position. It's speculation, but it makes sense, so I went with that explanation.

- So Panya Hassan did *not* try to sabotage the Americans as they were removing Cleopatra's

Needle from Egypt in 1880. But it's well documented that many Egyptians were angry that the obelisk was being taken away, even though the Egyptian government *gave* it to the U.S. as a gift. It's true that the Americans doing the work were hissed and cursed at in the streets of Alexandria. I don't know of any attempts to sabotage their efforts. I put that in for drama.

- So Thomas Brighton did *not* plug the leaky boiler with chewing gum or fix the broken crankshaft on the *Dessoug*. But the boiler on the *Dessoug did* spring a leak on the way to America. The crankshaft *did* break and had to be replaced. The *Dessoug did* encounter a storm that could have sent it to the bottom of the Atlantic Ocean. And chewing gum *did* first become popular during this time period.

- So Rebecca Watson did *not* invent the turntable that helped Cleopatra's Needle navigate the twists and turns in the streets of New York City. But it's true that it took six days to turn that first corner at 96th Street, and that after that a lazy Susan–type device was created to make the process of turning go much faster.

The story of Cleopatra's Needle is fascinating by itself. Why did I have to invent all those kids? The answer is simple—to make you want to read the book! To make the story more dramatic! That's what authors do. You probably wouldn't have picked up this book if it was just the history of some old monument you never heard of.

These kids and their diaries don't exist, but the rest of the story is real. Cleopatra's Needle really *was* carved in the granite quarries of Aswan, Egypt, in 1461 BCE and floated down the Nile to Heliopolis. Around 12 BCE, Augustus Caesar moved it to Alexandria, where it stood for almost two thousand years. Then it was brought to America the way I described it here.

I didn't make any of that stuff up. The information in this book came from many sources, especially Dr. Brier's book that I mentioned earlier and also Martina D'Alton's *The New York Obelisk, or, How Cleopatra's Needle Came to New York and What Happened When It Got Here.*

Another source was an 1882 book titled *Egyptian Obelisks* by Lieutenant Commander Henry Gorringe. He's the true hero of this story.

I live right near Central Park, and when I would ride my bike around the park, I would see Cleopatra's Needle and wonder what it was, how it got here, and who brought it. During the pandemic in 2020, I finally took the time to find the answers to these questions.

I learned that with the help of his assistants and workers, Henry Gorringe figured out how to lower a 222-ton obelisk in Egypt, buy a ship, get the obelisk into the ship, cross the Atlantic Ocean with it, drag it across New York City, and raise it where it stands today in Central Park. Along the way, he had to overcome enormous technical challenges, mechanical breakdowns, hostile enemies, harsh weather, and other obstacles. And he didn't have any kids to help him!

In fifteen months, he moved Cleopatra's Needle about 6,000 miles. He did it before cars, trucks, planes, or computers had been invented. And he did it for *free*! The $75,000 that William Vanderbilt offered him went to cover the expenses to do the job. In the end, it cost $103,732.

Henry Gorringe should be a national hero. But I'll bet you never heard of him before you read this book.

His story has a sad ending. After he finished his mission bringing Cleopatra's Needle to America, Henry Gorringe resigned from the Navy, went on a lecture tour, and wrote his book. Then, on July 7, 1885—just four years after his great accomplishment—Gorringe died in a freak accident. He was trying to board a moving train in Philadelphia when he slipped, fell, and hit his head. He was just forty-four years old. Maybe somebody *did* put a curse on him!

Gorringe is buried twenty-one miles from Cleopatra's Needle, at Rockland Cemetery in Sparkill, New York. Above his grave is a monument made from Vermont granite—a replica of Cleopatra's Needle, but without the hieroglyphics.

The gravesite of Lieutenant Commander Henry Honychurch Gorringe.

When Cleopatra's Needle arrived in America, it was a huge sensation. People came from all over to see it. Today, it seems kind of lonely, standing by itself in Central Park. Thousands of people walk, jog, and bike past it every day. But hardly any of them seem to notice this grand monument, which is now dwarfed by the city's skyscrapers. Many longtime New Yorkers have no idea what it is or how it got there. Tourists pay lots of money to go to the top of the Empire State Building. They wait in long lines to get into the Metropolitan Museum of Art. But hardly anybody walks around behind the museum to visit Cleopatra's Needle, which is totally free.

Today you can see obelisks of all sizes all over the world. Rome has more than any other city. In fact, an obelisk was discovered there in the sixteenth century by a barber digging a latrine behind his shop. Most of them are on city streets, in museums, and especially in cemeteries. They draw our eyes up to the sky and serve as symbols of endurance, eternity, immortality, and the power of the human spirit. They're a reminder that anything is possible.

ABOUT THE AUTHOR

Dan Gutman (seen here at Henry Gorringe's gravesite) has written many books for young readers, such as *Houdini and Me*, the My Weird School series, *The Genius Files, Flashback Four, The Kid Who Ran for President, The Million Dollar Shot,* and his Baseball Card Adventures series. Dan and his wife Nina live in New York City, across Central Park from Cleopatra's Needle. You can learn more about Dan and his books by visiting dangutman.com or following him on Facebook, Twitter/X, and Instagram.